The Last Battle: Yeoman
of the Third Reich
(A Sergeant Yeoman WWII Adventure)

Robert Jackson

Table of Contents

Chapter One

THE METEOR FIGHTER TURNED IN A LEISURELY CIRCLE FIVE miles over Salisbury Plain, the vapour trails from its twin turbojets inscribing a broad chalk mark across the cloudless April sky. The roar of the engines penetrated the cockpit only as a muted whisper, mingling with the soft sound of the airflow as it passed over the streamlined contours of the aircraft.

Wing Commander George Yeoman pushed the stick over to the left, dropping a wing and looking down at the greyish-green expanse of the plain far below. The roads that meandered across it were white, thread-like streaks, merging with the darker patches of towns. There, to the south of the little town of Larkhill, he could make out the great circle of Stonehenge, looking from this height no larger than the smallest coin, its monoliths casting short shadows in the morning sunlight.

It was a morning for rejoicing, for relaxing and soaking in the sun that burned through the perspex of the cockpit. Rarely, during the past five years, had Yeoman been able to enjoy moments such as this. From the time he had first joined an operational squadron in France on that fateful day in May 1940, as a very green young pilot officer, fate had tossed him across the face of Europe, from one embattled sky to another, until it had sometimes seemed to him that he no longer had the will or purpose to direct his own life, or to be master of even a tiny part of his own destiny.

Those five years had seen that twenty-year-old novice pilot turn into a hardened veteran with thirty-four victories to his credit, placing him among the RAF'S half-dozen top scorers. Death had brushed its dark wing across his face many times, and each time he had been given another chance; many of his closest friends had not been so fortunate.

Now, thank God, the long nightmare would soon be over. In these first days of April 1945, the last vestiges of German military might were being crushed to extinction by the relentless drive of the Allied armies. On 23 March, after a shattering bombardment by land and air, British and American forces had smashed their way across the Rhine north and south of Wesel, and the following morning their bridgehead had been reinforced by a massive airdrop of the 6th British and 17th us airborne divisions, overwhelming the desperate enemy opposition. Before the end of the month, the American 1st Army, further to the south, had burst out of its bridgehead at Remagen to join up with the forces near Wesel, isolating the industrial heart of Germany from the main body and trapping Feldmarschall Model's Army Group B in the Ruhr pocket. After that, the German armies everywhere in the west had begun to crumble away in disastrous retreat. The floodgates were open, and the great drive to Berlin was on.

According to the latest Intelligence reports, the American spearheads were only sixty miles from the shattered enemy capital — but the Russians were closer, and only the defensive line of the River Oder lay between them and the city. It could only be a matter of weeks, perhaps even days, before the end came.

Yeoman and his squadron, No. 505, had been away from the action for more than two months now. After flying Hawker Tempest Mk 5s — the fastest of all Allied fighters — from airfields in Holland during the bitter winter months, they had returned to England to re-equip with the RAF'S newest machines, Gloster Meteor jet fighters.

The first few Meteors had been hurriedly sent into action in the summer of 1944 against the German V-I flying bombs that were being launched against southern England, but their success had been far from spectacular. They had shot down only thirteen V-Is; Tempests, on the other hand, had destroyed over six hundred. It was, perhaps, not a fair comparison, because the Tempest was in service in greater numbers; but there was no escaping the fact that those early Meteor Mk IS were a good deal slower than the piston-engined Hawker fighter and that they had suffered their share of teething troubles, ranging from burnt-out engines to cannon jamming at altitude.

The Meteor Mk 3, however, was a different story. Fitted with more powerful engines than the Mk 1 — Rolls-Royce Derwents — it could reach a top speed of 493 mph at thirty thousand feet and could climb to forty-four thousand feet, although it was very sluggish and unresponsive at that altitude. It was armed with four 20-mm Hispano cannon in the nose and had a range of 1,300 miles.

The original Meteor squadron, No. 616, had now equipped with Mk 3s and was operating from a base in Holland, where it had been joined by a second Meteor unit, No. 504 Squadron. Both squadrons had been sent to the Continent to counteract the Luftwaffe's Messerschmitt 262 jet fighters, but as far as Yeoman knew they had made no contact with the Luftwaffe at all, the Meteors being employed on ground-attack operations.

Now, within the week, No. 505 Squadron was to go to the Continent too — but there was to be a difference. Unlike the other two Meteor units, No. 505 would be operating from the soil of Germany — from the newly-captured airfield of Rheine-Hopsten, in fact, to the north of Munster. In the Meteor's cockpit, Yeoman smiled to himself at the thought; in days gone by the thought of operating anywhere near Rheine had given Allied pilots nightmares, for it had been one of the top Luftwaffe fighter bases and consequently had been surrounded by flak. Rheine had come in for a lot of attention from 505 Squadron's Tempests during the closing weeks of 1944, as they sought to destroy the elusive Me 262 jets, and the airfield had taken a considerable battering. Operating from it would be no easy task; apart from its condition, the airfield would be right in the front line and the squadron might have to contend with saboteurs as well as with the Luftwaffe.

Unless, of course, the war ended by the time they reached Germany ... In sheer exuberence at the thought Yeoman rolled the Meteor a few times and then, pushing the nose down slightly to build up speed, pulled the fighter up into a loop. Shadows chased each other starkly over the instrument panel as the Meteor's nose pointed up into the blue and then, as the fighter curved over on to its back, the grey-green plain slid into view once more, passing over the top of the cockpit until the Meteor's nose was pointing vertically earthwards. The aircraft flashed through its own vapour trails and Yeoman gently brought it back to level flight again, feeling the 'g' forces pushing him into his seat as gravity fought a brief battle to pull him down, and lost.

A glance at the fuel gauges told him that it was time to go home. Home, for another few days at least, was the RAF airfield of Colerne, twenty-five miles away to the north-west. He turned on to a heading of 320 degrees and, throttling back to begin a leisurely descent, pressed the R/T transmit button on the control column.

'Muckheap, this is Thistle. Returning to base.' Whoever thought up this week's set of code names, he told himself, must be an amateur gardener.

'Roger, Thistle, Muckheap answering. Runway two-four, QFE one-zero-two-eight.'

Yeoman acknowledged and continued his descent, enjoying the scenery. By the time he passed over the old town of Melksham he was down to five thousand feet and dropping steadily towards the airfield, which was now less than ten miles away and clearly visible. At three miles out he called that he was on long final approach and made his cockpit checks; the green lights that showed the undercarriage was down and locked glowed at him reassuringly.

There was a fairly strong crosswind and Yeoman brought the Meteor crabbing down towards the runway at an angle, compensating for the drift. With flaps one-third down he crossed the airfield boundary at 100 knots; the runway threshold drifted under his wings and he eased back the stick slightly, his other hand on the throttles, at the same time kicking the rudder pedals to line up the Meteor's nose with the runway centreline in one smooth fluid movement.

The mainwheels touched with a slight jolt and he closed the throttles maintaining backward pressure on the stick until the nosewheel settled gently on to the concrete as the Meteor lost speed. The Meteor was the first tricycle-undercarriage aircraft Yeoman had flown, and landing it was a good deal less complicated than landing a tailwheel type such as the Tempest.

The twin Derwents whined as he opened the throttles once more, feeding in sufficient power to taxi the aircraft clear of the runway. Methodically he went through the after-landing checks; pneumatic pressure sufficient for taxi-ing; flaps up, selector neutral; air brakes closed.

No. 505 Squadron's fifteen Meteors were parked in a long line at the dispersal area near the hangars. With nothing to fear any more from the Luftwaffe, there was no longer any need to disperse the aircraft around the field. Looking ahead, Yeoman saw an airman standing at the end of the line, his arms raised, ready to marshall the Meteor into its place. He followed the man's directions and brought the fighter to a standstill, closing the high-pressure cock to cut off the fuel supply to the engine burners and shutting down the low-pressure pumps. The shrill whine of the Derwents dwindled and died as the turbines slowly stopped revolving.

Yeoman completed the rest of his checks and cranked back the cockpit canopy. He unfastened his seat and parachute harnesses, oxygen and microphone leads and climbed from the aircraft by way of the footsteps and handholds built into the port side of the front fuselage, jumping down on to the tarmac and wincing a little as he did so. Back in 1940, during the Battle of Britain, he had received some cannon shell fragments in his left foot; they had been successfully removed and the foot had given him no trouble until a few weeks ago, when it had inexplicably begun to throb whenever he put strong pressure on it. He had been meaning to see the MO about it for some time.

He nodded to the airman who had marshalled him in and made his way towards the flight-line hut to sign the Form 700, the aircraft technical log that recorded any snags. There had been none on this trip.

At a safe distance from the aircraft he paused to light his pipe, which he always carried with him, filled. As he did so, his thoughts turned once again to Rheine, and in particular to the man who, a few months ago, had commanded the Focke-Wulf and Messerschmitt squadrons of Fighter Wing 66, which had been 505 Squadron's main adversary.

Yeoman recalled the Intelligence profile of his opposite number. There had been a photograph attached to it, cut from a Swiss aviation magazine. It depicted a man of about Yeoman's own age, fair-haired and much decorated wearing a rather tired smile. It was strange, Yeoman had thought as he read the report, how Colonel Joachim Richter's career had run so closely parallel to his own.

Idly, he wondered what Richter was doing now — if he was still alive.

*

There was a time, earlier in the war, when Brandenburg airfield was a choice posting for a young Luftwaffe officer. Apart from the fact that the fleshpots of Berlin were less than forty miles away, there were unlimited shooting and fishing facilities in the picturesque countryside surrounding the airfield, and one could live the life of a country gentleman while still discharging one's duties to the full.

Now, in April 1945, Brandenburg was a smouldering wilderness. Continual Allied bombing had turned the surface of the airfield into a lunar landscape and the ancient stately homes in the neighbourhood, whose estates had offered so much in the way of sport, were locked and shuttered, their owners having fled to the safer climate of Bavaria.

A little Kubelwagen Kfz 1 — the German equivalent of America's famous Jeep — raced at high speed round Brandenburg's perimeter track, the driver expertly dodging the mounds of earth and broken concrete that surrounded the bomb craters. The air reeked of high explosive and the car's two occupants were red-eyed from the stinging, drifting smoke.

Major Hasso von Gleiwitz rested his hands lightly on the steering wheel, supremely confident of his ability to navigate the Kfz 1 round the obstacles in his path. Beside him, his passenger sat half-turned in the seat, his eyes continually scanning the sky above and behind. One never knew, these days, when a flight of Mustangs or Thunderbolts might drop down out of the clouds and make a lightning strafing attack, speeding away to safety before the flak had time to react.

Von Gleiwitz turned from the perimeter track on to a large area of unmarked concrete over which camouflage netting had been expertly draped thirty feet above the ground. The netting also concealed the entrance to a low hangar, built into a hillside and protected by massive blast-proof doors. He brought the vehicle to a halt in a small parking bay and switched off the engine, then reached behind him to retrieve his cap and gloves from the rear seat.

His companion stepped out of the car and paused for a moment, looking back across the devastated airfield.

'Listen, Hasso,' he said suddenly, 'can you hear anything?'

Von Gleiwitz looked at him enquiringly. Apart from the metallic ticking of the cooling car engine there was no sound.

'No, sir. Not a thing. Is something wrong?'

Colonel Joachim Richter shook his head and gave a weary smile. 'No, Hasso. I was just trying to remember when I last heard a bird sing. I expect the bombs have frightened them all away. Perhaps the birds have deserted Germany, Hasso.'

They walked to the mouth of a low, arched tunnel of reinforced concrete that ran for some distance along the side of the hangar and halted before a small steel door at the far end. Von Gleiwitz pressed a bell and a grille opened almost instantly, subjecting them to the intense scrutiny of a sentry. Then the door swung open on well-oiled hinges and they went into the building, Richter flicking a brief salute in the direction of the heavily-armed sentry who had slammed stiffly to attention.

After the comparative silence of the April morning, the noise inside the hangar seemed almost deafening. Somewhere in the background a generator hammered away, providing power for the rows of electric lights that glared down on the angular yet graceful lines of the Messerschmitt 262 jet fighters. There were nine of them, some camouflaged in mottled shades of dark and light grey, others still with the natural metal finish in which they had left the Messerschmitt factory. Mechanics were swarming over them like ants, making them ready for the next operational sortie.

Richter and von Gleiwitz walked quickly across the hangar, stepping carefully over electrical cables, and passed through a door at the far side. A flight of steps led them down to yet another door, giving access to a room set into the ground about fifteen feet below the level of the hangar itself.

The room was dominated by a large table on which a map of northern Germany was spread, protected by a sheet of perspex. There was a lot of equipment in the room — radio transceivers, telephones and so on — but most of it was useless. Only one telephone afforded contact with the outside world, being a direct line to the 4th Air Division's underground control room at Döberitz, near Berlin.

Twelve pilots were standing or sitting around the big table. Those who were seated moved quickly to rise as Richter entered, but he just as quickly motioned to them to stay where they were.

They were all desperately tired, and needed all the rest they could get. He could not remember when he had last enjoyed a good night's sleep; even pills did not block out the recurrent nightmares that were brought on by extreme tension and over-exhaustion. Hunger and thirst were a part of their daily lives, too; a diet of little more than black bread and sausage did nothing to improve a man's strength and morale, while the water supply was more often than not disrupted by the bombing.

It was therefore in the nature of a miracle when one of the officers, Major Dauer, produced two tin mugs half-filled with a hot liquid which Richter and von Gleiwitz, on testing it cautiously, discovered to be genuine coffee. Richter took a mouthful, rolled it carefully round his tongue and let it trickle down his throat, resisting the temptation to swallow it all in one go.

'My God, Georg,' he said to the smiling Dauer, 'where did you get hold of this?'

'You have my batman to thank, sir,' the other answered. 'He'd apparently been hoarding it away for ages, and decided that now was the time to produce it. That's the last of it, though, now we've all had a taste,' he added regretfully.

Richter sighed and set down his mug on the table top. It was covered with a layer of gritty dust, as was everything else in the room.

A sudden thud shook the room, causing more dust to shower down. Everyone flinched and ducked instinctively, then looked at one another, somewhat embarrassed.

The explosion had been nothing more than a dud bomb, detonated by a disposal squad somewhere beyond the airfield perimeter. Richter wondered if the squad had been blown up with the weapon; all sorts of people were being put to work on bomb disposal and airfield repair work nowadays, and gangs of starved wretches in tattered uniforms of the Todt Organization's forced labour deportees had become a familiar sight as they toiled to repair the surface of Brandenburg field in the wake of a raid, urged on by the machine-pistols of merciless SS guards.

Even the pilots, and Richter was no exception, had come to accept the presence of such unfortunate creatures as a necessary evil, distasteful though it was. Without the forced labour gangs, the bomb craters on the runways would never be filled in, for no troops were available to do the job, and consequently the fighters would be unable to operate. Some of the forced labourers died, of course — quite a lot, in fact, so Richter understood — but then they would probably die anyway, in the long run, because when the inevitable collapse came it was unlikely that their SS guards would permit them to survive. In the meantime, they were performing a useful function, their labours assisting young men to murder other young men for a lost and worthless cause.

Ritcher surveyed the assembled pilots. Not one of them was below the rank of captain; their decorations and the tension-lines on their young-old faces testified to their experience in combat.

This, then, was all that remained of Fighter Wing 66, the unit in which he had cut his teeth in action and now, nearly six years later, had returned to command in its last battles. Fourteen men, including himself and von Gleiwitz, and nine Messerschmitt 262s — the 'wonder fighter' that had come too late to save Germany from the avalanche of Allied bombers.

Richter had long since given up speculating what might have happened if the Messerschmitt 262 had entered service with the Luftwaffe in the middle of 1943, in time to smash Allied air superiority before the middle of the following year, when the Anglo-American armies invaded Europe. The 262 had been about to enter production as a fighter when Hitler had insisted on the jets being converted to carry bombs for use as a 'reprisal weapon', and as a result there had been months of delay before the first aircraft begun to roll off the production lines. German fighter pilots, therefore, tended to blame Hitler for the fact that the 262 had not been available in sufficient numbers to help stem the Allied onslaught, but Richter knew that the truth was not quite as simple. There had been technical problems, too, which had taken a long time to sort out.

The design of the Messerschmitt was superb, with graceful, clean lines and all the latest aero-dynamic refinements. It was its turbojet engines that had let it down. The Junkers Jumo 004 turbines had been rushed into production far too soon, with the result that some of the prototype 262s had suffered serious accidents when their engines exploded in mid-air. The snags had not all been ironed out even now, in the spring of 1945. Only the other day, a 262's engine had blown up as the aircraft was climbing away from Brandenburg, tearing off a wing and killing the pilot.

In the operations room there was little talking. Richter and his pilots waited, smoking nervously, glancing at the wall clock from time to time. The Americans were late today; usually, the order to take off had been received by this time.

Von Gleiwitz left the room briefly, returning with the news that the Messerschmitts were being pulled up the ramp from the underground hangar and lined up on the concrete apron outside, where they were being fuelled and armed. The antiaircraft batteries around the airfield were on the alert, ready to deal with any marauding fighter-bombers.

It couldn't be long now. The pilots pulled on their one-piece black leather flying overalls, picked up their helmets and, on Richter's orders, went out to their fighters and strapped themselves into the cockpits. This was a difficult enough procedure in itself, for the 262 was fitted with an ejection seat and the pilot wore a special parachute pack which, when strapped on, formed a kind of seat cushion that extended from shoulders to buttocks, and unless he took great care when strapping himself in the pack and harness could become extremely uncomfortable.

Ritcher sat with the cockpit canopy open, his helmet on his knee, impatiently drumming his fingertips against the metal of the fuselage side. His ground crew stood beside the auxiliary starter motor, waiting expectantly.

They did not have to wait for long. An orderly, who had been standing watch by the operations room telephone, came running from the hangar and sprinted across to Richter's aircraft, handing the pilot a slip of paper. Richter glanced at it quickly: nearly two hundred B-17 Flying Fortresses, with a strong fighter escort, had crossed the coast of northern Germany at an altitude of twenty-five thousand feet and were following a heading which, unless they changed it in the next few minutes, would take them to Berlin.

Richter tossed the scrap of paper aside and raised his arm, moving his hand in a circular motion. The ground crew went into action at once, plugging the two-stroke auxiliary motor into the intake of the port turbine. The engine began to turn slowly, then accelerated in fits and starts. Richter waited until the rpm reached 4,000 and then opened the throttle slowly, feeling his heart leap as the motor gave a sudden loud bang. He glanced hastily at the jet exhaust to see if there was any sign of flames, but the turbine settled down into a steady, screaming whine and he opened the fuel cock fully until the 262 shuddered to the engine's pulsing, throbbing roar. The ground crew repeated the process with the starboard engine and soon both power units were running, the pilot keeping a watchful eye on the fuel pressures and juggling with the throttles until the rpm of both turbines were synchronized. Behind the 262, a long swathe of grass burned and smoked in the hot jet exhaust; the air stank of paraffin vapour.

Richter, who had already pulled on his helmet to protect his ears against the roar of the motors, now swung the cockpit canopy into place and locked it. He looked around and noted with satisfaction that the engines of the other 262s were emitting long trails of shimmering exhaust gases; for once, it seemed to have been a trouble-free start.

He waved to the ground crew, who quickly pulled away the chocks, and carefully opened the throttles until the 262 began to move forward. He taxied slowly over the rough uneven surface of the perimeter track, taking care not to move too fast in case the turbines overheated and also to permit the ground crew, who were jogging alongside, to keep up with him; their assistance was usually necessary to line up the fighter on the runway, as there was no airflow from a propeller to make the rudder effective for steering the aircraft on the ground. Turning had to be achieved by using the brakes, and it was all too easy to burn them out.

The 262s formed up on the runway in threes, von Gleiwitz and Dauer lining up alongside Richter's aircraft with the aid of their mechanics, who pushed hard on the trailing edges of the wings, deafened by the screech of the turbines. Then the ground crew scattered, running clear of the runway. The corporal in charge of Richter's crew, a lanky red-haired man from the Moabit district of Berlin, gave the pilot an informal salute and shook a fist at the sky a gesture that meant: knock hell out of the bastards. Richter knew that the corporal's home had been flattened by American bombs a few weeks earlier.

The noise of the turbines rose to a pounding roar as Richter eased forward the twin throttles. The first section of three jets gathered speed slowly, lurching from time to time as their undercarriages passed over newly-filled bomb craters. From the corner of his eye, Richter caught a glimpse of a group of forced labourers in their miserable striped rags, gazing dumbly at the Messerschmitts as they howled past.

The rpm gauge showed 8,000 and the speed built up steadily, the needle of the airspeed indicator flicking past the 240 km/h mark. The jet was eating up the runway, but it was heavily laden with full fuel tanks, full magazines of 30-mm cannon shells and twenty-four 50-mm R4M air-to-air rockets, the latter fitted in racks under the wings, and was reluctant to leave the ground.

The end of the runway was coming up fast and the whole airframe was rattling and shaking. The airspeed indicator showed nearly 300 km/h. Richter eased back the stick and the nosewheel lifted a few inches off the ground, only to drop back again with a thud. There was only one thing for it. Quickly he reached down and pulled the lever that changed the angle of incidence of the tailplane, performing the same action as a trimming wheel on a more conventional aircraft. Instantly, the rumbling and jolting ceased as the fighter rotated on the axis of its mainwheels and staggered into the air.

Richter fought to keep the wings level as the 262 crossed the airfield boundary at just above stalling speed. The controls were sloppy and the aircraft kept on trying to drop a wing as the struggling, underpowered turbojets fought to develop sufficient thrust to overcome weight and drag.

The pilot raised the undercarriage and flaps, and the effect was dramatic. The speed increased rapidly now and the 262 became a clean aerodynamic shape, like the swallow-Schwalbe — after which it was named. Richter held it down until the airspeed indicator showed 720 km/h and then pulled back the stick, putting the fighter into a steady climb.

Von Gleiwitz and Dauer were keeping station with him and a glance behind told him that the other six 262s had all taken off safely and were also climbing to join the formation. He pressed the R/T transmit button and called up the fighter control station near the German capital. 'Albatross, this is Elbe. Instructions please.'

Richter had been using 'Elbe' as his personal callsign for three years now, and had persistently refused to change it. The very fact that it must be very familiar to the British and Americans by now gave him a grim personal satisfaction; he liked them to know who was hunting them.

Receiving no reply, he called again. This time, the response was immediate.

'Elbe, this is Albatross. Fat Dogs now in sector Friedrich-Wolfgang one-three, altitude seven-five-zero-zero metres. Steer two-nine-zero.'

Richter acknowledged curtly and led the formation round to the new heading, climbing all the time. The reference given by the fighter controller meant that the enemy bombers were now between Hamburg and Hannover, somewhere over Lüneburg Heath. They seemed to be heading for Berlin, all right.

Richter made a rapid mental calculation. If the Messerschmitts maintained their present speed in the climb, the pilots should sight the enemy formation in just over five minutes. It would not give the 262s much time to get above the bombers and manoeuvre into a favourable attack position; the pilots would just have to do the best they could.

Richter led the nine jets up to twenty-eight thousand feet and they levelled out at that altitude, leaving broad white swathes of vapour behind them as they sped across the sky at over 500 mph. They could see the enemy now, crawling up out of the haze that shrouded the western horizon; a solid phalanx of bombers, with the thinner vapour trails of the fighter escort slashing their path in groups of twelve above and on either flank.

The fighter escort was flying higher than Richter had expected. He ordered the jets up to thirty-three thousand, well clear of the opposition, and quickly took stock of the situation.

The nine Messerschmitt 262s, in their three elements of three aircraft, were nicely spaced out, with three hundred yards between each element and about 150 yards between individual aircraft. Richter ordered them to alter course to the right, so that they would pass above and to one side of the American formation; the 262 needed plenty of room to turn and this manoeuvre would make it easier for the jets to curve behind the enemy. Almost dispassionately, he noted that some of the American fighter groups were altering course too, climbing to place themselves between the jets and the bombers, but the German pilots could afford to ignore them; the 262 was a good 100 mph faster than either the P-47 Thunderbolt or the P-51 Mustang, the two main USAAF escort types, and unless the jets were forced to slow down during combat manoeuvres the piston-engined fighters stood no chance of catching them.

The jet fighter pilots could identify the enemy aircraft clearly now. The bombers were B-17 Flying Fortresses and the escorting fighters were, as Richter had suspected, Mustangs. As the 262s swept past to starboard, well out of range of the bombers' heavy Armament of ten 0.5-inch machine guns per aircraft, Richter saw one group of Mustangs release its auxiliary fuel tanks, which fluttered down towards the German countryside like a shower of metallic rain.

He saw, too, that there were gaps in one or two of the bomber formations; flak and fighters had already claimed some victims. He had no doubt, though, that the swarming Mustangs had quickly overwhelmed the dwindling numbers of piston-engined fighters that the Luftwaffe was still capable of hurling into the battle.

Assessing the situation rapidly, Richter selected a box of fifteen bombers that was bringing up the rear of the American formation and warned his pilots that he proposed to attack it. A glance around assured him that there was no immediate threat from the Mustangs and he brought the nine 262s round in a wide curve until they were flying on the same heading as the bombers, but several miles astern and still a couple of thousand metres higher up.

The use of the speedy jet fighters had brought about a complete revision of Luftwaffe fighter tactics, for the Messerschmitt 262's high speed made the tactics usually adopted by the Luftwaffe's piston-engined fighters — a frontal attack followed by a half roll and then a steep dive away — completely out of the question. Richter therefore began his attack approach from a distance of five thousand metres astern of the bombers, the jets still flying in three flights of three, each flight a few hundred metres behind the other.

Richter and his two wingmen put their aircraft into a shallow dive, building up speed steadily until the airspeed indicators showed 850 km/h and levelling out fifteen hundred metres behind the rearmost box of Fortresses. Richter selected a Fortress in the centre of the group; it seemed to leap towards him, shrouded in a grey haze of smoke from its own guns.

The pilot hunched up in his seat, ignoring the machine-gun fire that streamed towards him, and concentrated on the bulk of the enemy bomber as it grew larger between the luminous dots of his Revi gunsight. As an extra aiming guide, two parallel lines were etched on the jet fighter's windscreen; when the Fortress's wingspan filled the space between them, Richter knew that the range would be exactly six hundred metres.

His thumb caressed the firing button. He was careful not to make any sudden control movements, for at this speed a jerky hand on the stick could cause the 262 to skid wildly.

For an instant, as the bomber loomed up in front of him, he had the wild sensation that he had lost control of everything, and that he was doomed to plunge on until he smashed himself and his fighter to oblivion against the enemy. Then the fleeting moment passed, and his nerves were once more rock-steady. Savagely, he jabbed his thumb down on the button.

The full salvo of twenty-four R4M rockets swished from their rails under the 262's wings in three-tenths of a second. With incredible speed the missiles sped towards their target, glowing coals trailing black plumes of smoke, fanning out like a spread of pellets from a shotgun cartridge to cover the whole silhouette of the big four-engined bomber.

The effect was terrifying. The Fortress, pulverized by at least half the R4M salvo, simply disintegrated in a great ball of smoke and fire out of which aluminium fragments whirled. The explosion was so vast that it encompassed a neighbouring bomber, tearing away a wing and leaving the carcass to spin ponderously down.

There was no time to see any more. Richter pulled back the stick and the 262 streaked like a grey blur over the top of the Fortress formation, closing fast on the group ahead. The pilot singled out another Fortress, flying on the left-hand side of the box, and opened fire with four 30-mm Mk 108 cannon, seeing the shells burst with a flash and a puff of smoke on the bomber's starboard wing. Instantly, a sheet of blazing fuel poured back, licking along the fuselage side. The stricken wing dropped and the big bomber fell away into a spiral dive. As he sped overhead, Richter noted that at least one of the Fortress's gunners was still firing at him.

Richter pulled back the stick and sent the 262 rocketing skywards in a vertical climb, bursting through a group of Mustangs. The American fighters scattered in all directions and Richter ignored them, knowing that they could never catch him in the climb. He levelled out and looked down; as he suspected, the Mustangs were still trying to sort themselves out and he selected one that was some distance away from the rest, waggling its wings uncertainly as though its pilot was not sure of his bearings.

The American clearly had no eyes for the danger above him. Richter came down on him like a hawk, levelling out astern and opening fire as the Mustang drifted into the luminous circle of his gunsight. His first burst was right on target and he saw large pieces break off the enemy fighter, followed by a plume of white smoke. The transparent cockpit canopy flew off, but Richter had no time to see whether the pilot baled out. His high speed swept him past the shattered Mustang and he dived away, the white trails from his turbines showing threads of black as he opened the throttles, speeding clear of all pursuit in a shallow dive.

His fuel reserves were running low and it was time to head for home. He called up the other 262s and they joined him one by one, the pilots chattering excitedly over the R/T. Every one of them had scored a victory, and Richter felt elation sweep through him as he mentally added up the score. Ten bombers and four fighters wiped out in a single attack by only nine jets; if only the 262s had been available in their hundreds!

The nine jet fighters returned to Brandenburg without incident; for once, the sky was clear of enemy fighters and the 262s were able to land unmolested. By the time vengeful American fighter-bombers braved Brandenburg's intense anti-aircraft fire to strafe the airfield, the 262s were safely underground and the attackers found what appeared to be a deserted field, its surface pock-marked like the face of the moon. The Mustangs made a single run over the airfield, found nothing of interest, then flew away to rejoin the armada of Flying Fortresses, now winging its way back to England.

The German fighter controllers had been wrong. Instead of spearing on to Berlin, the Fortresses had swung south and unloaded their bombs on the already devastated railway yards of Magdeburg. As the bombers droned away, they were attacked by small groups of piston-engined Focke-Wulfs and Messerschmitts, hurriedly thrown into the fray from their airfields near Hannover. Overwhelmed by the Mustangs, the German fighters stood no real chance; the blazing wrecks of thirty-five of them marked the Americans' passage across the countryside. For the Luftwaffe, April 1945 was a bloody twilight.

Chapter Two

'JESUS,' YEOMAN MUTTERED, LOOKING AROUND HIM. 'WHAT a dump.'

It was Friday, the thirteenth of April, and the Meteors of No. 505 Squadron, their pilots scorning all superstition, had just landed at Rheine after flying out from Colerne, stopping once to refuel at Nijmegen.

'You should have seen it when we got here,' the young officer beside Yeoman remarked cheerfully. He was a flight lieutenant in the Royal Air Force Regiment, the specialist force which, formed in 1942 to protect RAF airfields, had performed sterling service during these early months of 1945, its armoured car squadrons often pushing ahead of the British army to capture key enemy airfields and hold them while they were made usable for the aircraft of the 2nd Tactical Air Force, operating close to the front line.

'You couldn't see the runways for holes,' the flight lieutenant continued, 'and the whole place was a sea of mud. A lot of the installations were still in one piece, though, including the officers' mess. Jump in, sir, and I'll take you there now.' He indicated the jeep that stood nearby, its engine running.

Yeoman nodded, dropped his parachute and flying helmet into the back of the vehicle, then turned to look at the newly-arrived Meteors, which were being towed into sandbagged and camouflaged dispersals under the supervision of Warrant Officer Logan, the NCO in charge of the squadron's ground crews. The latter had arrived at Rheine a day earlier, together with the squadron's supporting equipment, after an overland trek by convoy from Antwerp. Satisfied that all was well, he climbed into the jeep beside the flight lieutenant, noting that a truck was doing the rounds of the dispersals to pick up the other pilots.

Yeoman lit his pipe and relaxed as the jeep moved off, the driver keeping to the wire mesh that had been laid by engineers to form a taxi strip; the original taxiway had long since been blasted to pieces by Allied bombing. Looking out across the field with a professional eye, the wing commander saw the aggressive outlines of several Hawker Tempest fighter-bombers dispersed around the far side: they must belong to the squadrons of No. 122 Wing, which had moved up to Rheine from Holland at the beginning of the month. He noted, too, that the anti-aircraft guns around the airfield were well positioned; no doubt the RAF Regiment gunners had sited their weapons in the same places as their German predecessors, in order to provide a thick umbrella of shellfire over the runways and the approaches to the field.

The jeep turned off the taxiway and Yeoman looked up as a section of Tempests whistled overhead and joined the airfield circuit, their wheels and flaps lowered. He felt a pang that was almost one of nostalgia, for in the months when 505 Squadron had flown the big, powerful fighters he had come almost to love them, to revel in the vibration of the controls as the Tempest's slender wings sliced through the air at close on 500 mph, to exult in the tremendous power of the aircraft's four 20-mm cannon, unleashed at the touch of his thumb.

The Meteor was a different machine altogether. Looking back on his first flight in a jet, Yeoman supposed that he ought to have said something historic such as 'Well, here comes a new era in the story of man's endeavour to fly,' or something like that, but he had neither said nor thought anything of the kind. In fact, after the potent Tempest, the Meteor had come as something of a disappointment — until one got used to it, and realized that here was an aircraft whose development potential far exceeded anything that had preceded it.

Anyway, here he was, in command of the first Allied jet fighter unit to operate from the soil of Germany, right up in the front line with fifteen Meteors and a bunch of the most experienced fighter pilots the RAF had to offer. It was a pity, he reflected, that he had not had the chance to take the Meteors into action six months earlier, when the Luftwaffe was still very much in evidence; as it was, he feared that the squadron might not have much opportunity to see combat before the enemy's inevitable collapse.

The jeep cruised on past hangars and other installations, about fifty per cent of them damaged to some extent. Yeoman saw that the undamaged hangars were unoccupied, and asked the flight lieutenant why this was so.

'Too dangerous,' the man told him. 'Their structures have taken a bit of a pounding from near misses and a sudden explosion could cause the whole lot to fall apart. Only last week, the bomb disposal chaps were detonating some unexploded bombs on the edge of the airfield; the concussion took one of the big hangar doors clean off its mountings and it fell on top of an airman who happened to be walking past at the time. Squashed him completely flat.'

'Nice thought,' Yeoman muttered, casting a wary eye at a large hangar as they drove by.

'There were quite a few booby traps around the place when we first arrived, too,' the flight lieutenant remarked matter-of-factly. 'We lost a couple of blokes who decided to go poking around wrecked Jerry aircraft, looking for souvenirs. Blew themselves sky-high. They should have known better.' His tone was unsympathetic.

The dangerous hangars fell behind and the jeep turned left on to an arrow-straight road, flanked by rows of poplars, that led towards what was presumably the airfield's main gate. The latter was overlooked by a guardhouse, not unlike a standard pattern RAF guardroom, but consisting of two storeys instead of one. Grinning, red-faced British soldiers, rifles slung over their shoulders, waved the vehicle through without ceremony. Yeoman remarked that they looked happy.

'I suppose it's because they know we're on the last lap,' the flight lieutenant said, 'and that the war will be over very soon. They're Black Watch, and they had a hell of a time in the Reichswald battle a few weeks ago. They deserve a rest, poor devils.'

'Where's the operations room?' Yeoman wanted to know.

'It's in the officers' mess, sir. Or rather, in an annexe built on the end of it. It was the Group Captain's idea, and it works pretty well. If there's a "flap" on, no time is wasted getting word to the pilots, because the sergeant pilots share the mess too. Everyone gets a briefing on the spot and then they all pile into a couple of trucks and are dropped at their aircraft.'

Yeoman grunted, and nodded his approval. He had met the officer appointed as Rheine's station commander once before, briefly, while attending a course at the Day Fighter Leaders' School in Northumberland, and Group Captain Kingston had struck him immediately as a man who was in the habit of making the right decisions. As far as he knew, Kingston — one of the few fighter pilots, like himself, who had survived the war since those hectic days of the Battle of France — had commanded a Wing of Spitfires in Belgium before being promoted and moved on into Germany.

The officers' mess at Rheine turned out to be quite a palatial building, surrounded by trees and set amid beautifully landscaped gardens which were now sadly in need of attention, but upon which someone had obviously once lavished a great deal of loving care. Several drab military vehicles were parked outside, and there were armed sentries at the entrance. These were the only evidence of war, apart from the fact that the windows of the mess had been criss-crossed with adhesive tape as a protection against blast.

The two men climbed from the jeep and walked up the steps that led to the entrance, the sentries shouldering their rifles and slapping the butts in salute as the officers approached. Yeoman returned their compliment and pushed his way through the revolving door, finding himself in a spacious foyer whose centrepiece was a large mahogany table. The duty NCO, a corporal, looked up from the newspaper he had been reading, caught sight of the three rows of rank braid on Yeoman's battledress epaulettes and jumped to attention, a posture that was somewhat marred by a pencil stuck behind the man's ear.

Yeoman told the corporal to relax and walked up to the table to sign the 'warning-in' book, the reception register that is a feature of every RAF mess. As he did so, his eye happened to fall on the newspaper which the NCO had dropped hurriedly. It was a copy of the *Daily Mirror*, flown into Rheine on the duty Anson mail aircraft only a couple of hours earlier, and the headline stopped Yeoman in his tracks: ROOSEVELT DIES ON EVE OF ALLIED TRIUMPHS.

He snatched up the paper and scanned it quickly. 'President Roosevelt', he read, 'died suddenly from a cerebral haemorrhage in his sleep at West Springs, Georgia, yesterday afternoon. A White House statement said: "Vice President Truman has been notified ... " '

'Good God! That's a bit unexpected!' The exclamation came from the flight lieutenant, who had been reading over Yeoman's shoulder.'

The latter nodded soberly. 'Yes. I wonder what effect it will have on the war — whether it will make it drag out, if the Germans take fresh heart.' He frowned. 'I wonder what this chap Truman is like?'

The flight lieutenant shook his head slowly. 'Don't know, sir. Never heard of him. It seems an awful shame, with peace negotiations just around the corner.'

Yeoman made no further comment, lapsing into a thoughtful mood which, however, quickly lifted as the flight lieutenant took him on a conducted tour of the mess building. It was a pre-war structure, one of those built with the massive expansion of the Luftwaffe after the Nazis came to power in Germany and tore the Treaty of Versailles to shreds, and Yeoman could easily see why young men in their thousands had flocked to Hitler's banner with the promise of this kind of lifestyle. The dining-room was enormous and exquisitely panelled, with a minstrels' gallery at one end, and was clearly modelled on the style of a baronial banqueting hall; from it, a marble staircase wound its way down to a beer cellar, its walls covered with murals that depicted the whole story of Hitler's Luftwaffe, from the first clandestine flying schools that had been formed in the 1930s under the guise of gliding clubs to the involvement of the Condor Legion in Spain, with bombs showering down from painted Heinkels to pulverize Spanish towns, their agony captured forever by the unknown artist.

'Part of the story's missing,' Yeoman growled. 'The bit between 1939 and now, I mean. I reckon we could paint a few pictures of our own to complete the job.'

He paused, sniffing the air curiously like a hound investigating a strange scent. 'What's that funny smell?' he asked. 'It's like cheap perfume. In fact, this whole place smells like a whore's boudoir.'

The flight lieutenant grinned. 'That's not a bad description. It *is* perfume. Eau de cologne, to be precise. Apparently the Jerries use a lot of it, and the scent tends to linger on. I've noticed it before, in places they've recently vacated.' Yeoman wrinkled his nose. 'The place could do with a bloody good scrub down,' he muttered, turning back towards the stairway. 'Come on, let's see the rest of it.'

For Yeoman, used to the relatively austere atmosphere of an RAF mess, the tour of its German counterpart turned out to be quite an education. Not the least of the surprises came in the lavatory next door to the beer cellar, where the flight lieutenant showed Yeoman a line of porcelain basins, rather like wash-basins but smaller, each one with a large hole in the bottom and no plug. On either side of the basins were chromium handles, which were obviously meant to be gripped.

'They're for spewing-up in,' the flight lieutenant explained. 'The idea is that if you get a bellyful of beer, you come in here, stick a finger down your throat to get rid of it, then stagger back in for more.'

Yeoman made no comment. In a way he could see the sense behind the idea, but the fact that the Germans considered it necessary somehow made them seem more barbaric and alien.

The flight lieutenant showed Yeoman to his room, the two men passing through the foyer again and pushing their way past a noisy group of newly-arrived pilots, the latter clustered round the reception table while the harrassed corporal checked his list and told each one where he was to be accommodated. Arriving at his room, Yeoman was delighted to find that his kit, which had gone on ahead of him, had already been stowed neatly away by his batman, the astonishing and utterly efficient McGann, whose accent was completely unintelligible to anyone but his wing commander and who, plucked from a hard and precarious existence in the slums of Glasgow by the war, now seemed to have found a true purpose in life in looking after Yeoman, whom he regarded (much to the pilot's embarrassment) as a superior being a short step down the ladder from the Son of God.

Following the flight lieutenant's directions, Yeoman left the mess by a side door and headed for the annexe, to report to the group captain. As he made his way round the side of the main building, half a dozen Tempests passed overhead with a shattering roar, climbing hard towards the east, and Yeoman stood and watched them for a moment as they dwindled into the distance, heading for enemy territory. They would, he guessed, be looking primarily for enemy jets, which now represented the only real challenge to the swarming Allied air forces. He knew the system well; the Tempests would split up into pairs and cruise around on the approaches to airfields which the jets were known to be using, intent on catching the 262s as they slipped into land.

At the door to the annexe, over which someone had mounted a hastily-painted sign that said 'Operations', he was stopped by a sentry who demanded to see his identity documents. Satisfied, the man saluted and let Yeoman pass through into a lengthy corridor, with rooms on either side.

They had originally been bedrooms, designed to accommodate the over spill from the main mess building, but the bedroom furniture had all been thrown out and replaced by austere, RAF stores standard-issue type tables and chairs.

The whole building echoed with the clatter of typewriters and the shrilling of telephone bells. Yeoman stuck his head through a door marked 'Orderly Room' and asked a sergeant where he might find the group captain; the latter's office, he was told, was on the left at the far end of the corridor.

A crisp 'Come in' answered Yeoman's knock and he went inside, saluting the station commander. The latter held a telephone in one hand; with the other, he waved Yeoman towards a vacant chair. Gazing idly around the room, Yeoman's attention was taken by a large painting, hanging behind Kingston. It depicted a Wellington bomber of the RAF being shot down by a Messerschmitt 110 night-fighter. He was still looking at it when the group captain replaced the receiver and sat back in his chair, smiling at the newcomer.

'Quite a pretty picture, don't you think? Kingston said. 'We found it on one of the former Hun crew-rooms and there was a big argument among the 122 Wing boys as to which squadron should have it, so I settled the dispute by confiscating it.'

Kingston rose suddenly and stretched out a welcoming hand to Yeoman. 'Good to have you and your boys with us, George. I remember you very well from the Fighter Leader's course. Later on, we'll take half an hour off and you can show me over one of your Meteors; I haven't had the opportunity to see one at close quarters yet.'

Yeoman studied the group captain closely as he spoke. Kingston was a big, powerful man, with a square face and shoulders that filled the fabric of his tunic to bursting point. One of his bushy eyebrows seemed to be perpetually raised and this, together with the fact that his nose was slightly twisted, gave him a curiously loP-sided appearance. He picked up a pencil and fiddled with it, then looked hard at Yeoman and frowned. 'George, I may as well give you the bad news straight away. I've had a signal from Group, forbidding any operations by your Meteors over enemy-held territory. Instead, your squadron is to be used for airfield defence.'

He held up his hand as Yeoman started to protest. 'It's no use, George. Group is quite adamant. I don't know how long the restriction will last, and you may be sure that I'll do my best to have it lifted. In the meantime, I'm afraid you're stuck with local area patrols, and I don't want any of your boys swanning off over the other side and getting themselves shot down.'

Yeoman tried hard to mask his disappointment. 'I don't understand, sir,' he complained. 'The war's nearly over. Even if we did have the misfortune to lose a Meteor over enemy territory, it couldn't possibly be of any technical significance to the Huns at this stage. I thought the whole idea was to try out the aircraft in action against the 262s.'

Kingston looked at him for a few moments, tapping his pencil on the desk top. Then he said:

'I don't suppose it will do any harm to tell you the real reason, but for God's sake keep it to yourself. The truth is, we aren't worried about a Meteor falling into German hands — but we don't want the Russians to get hold of one. The less they know about our jet engines, the better; at least that seems to be the general feeling in the Air Ministry.'

Yeoman raised an eyebrow. 'But I thought the Russians were supposed to be our allies,' he said.

Kingston gave a short laugh. 'So they are, George. So they are. But for how long is anybody's guess, once this little lot is over, and there's no sense in giving away secrets to them. I might as well tell you that relations between ourselves and the Russians are balanced on a knife-edge, and have been for some time, despite what the newspapers say, and things are likely to become even more tense when we finally carve up Germany between us. We can't risk giving the Russians any kind of advantage at this stage.' Yeoman nodded. 'It all begins to make sense. Still, I hope we do have a chance to take a crack at the Huns before the end, otherwise the next few weeks are going to be a bit gloomy.'

The station commander grunted. 'Well, there it is, and there's not much we can do about it. Now then, let me give you the rest of the picture.

'First of all, the Huns have plenty of aircraft left. Make no mistake about that. Most of their pilots are not up to much, though, because they're scraping the bottom of the barrel. Nevertheless, there's a hard core of "old pros" who are very, very good indeed, and they are concentrated in the jet squadrons.

'I might add,' the group captain went on, 'that the 262s are becoming more and more hard to find. Just about all the big Luftwaffe airfields on the other side of the Elbe have been made unusable by bombing, and reconnaissance has shown no activity on them for some time. However, the Huns have perfected a new dispersal technique, using a lot of secondary fields, most of which have been built in the last year or so. Their runways are about fifteen hundred yards long and they are well camouflaged, the aircraft and equipment being hidden in nearby pine forests.

'The enemy fighter squadrons rotate between these bases, remaining at one location for not more than five days before moving on. They move their ground support equipment and personnel by night and the fighters arrive at dawn, so that they can be fuelled up in time to take off and intercept the first bombing raids of the day.'

Kingston got up, stretched like a big cat, and began pacing up and down the room, his hands clasped behind his back.

'The problem is,' he continued, 'that even when we succeed in locating these airfields, they are very difficult and dangerous targets to attack — but attacked they must be, because fighter-bombers operating from them are inflicting quite severe damage on our supply convoys and the Army is, understandably, screaming blue murder for the air force to do something about it. No. 2 Group's medium bombers can't help, because they are already stretched to the limit, and 84 Group can't help either, because their fighter-bombers are based too far to the rear. So that leaves us, in 83 Group, to carry the can. Our units, particularly the Tempest squadrons, have been devoting most of their time to carrying out low-level strafes on these airfields, and I don't mind telling you it's sheer bloody murder. One Tempest squadron lost eight aircraft out of eleven last week.'

'Flak?' Yeoman queried.

'Christ, yes, flak! According to our Intelligence boys, each of these secondary airfields is defended by a flak detachment consisting of one 37-mm battery and two 20-mm. The 37-mm battery comprises nine guns and the 20-mm battery twenty-four, in double-or quadruple-barrel mountings. The batteries are attached to the various enemy fighter Wings and follow them around — or, rather, they precede them, being very well installed by the time the Huns fly in. Together, the guns can put up about two hundred and fifty shells a second, and you can imagine what it's like running the gauntlet of that lot.'

Yeoman nodded grimly. Airfield flak had claimed a good many of his friends over the past couple of years, and he himself had narrowly escaped with his life on more than one occasion.

'What about anti-flak Typhoons?' he asked, referring to the deadly fighter-bombers of No. 84 Group, whose salvoes of rockets could pulverize anything from a flak post to a battle cruiser. 'Can't they help?'

'They help when they can,' Kingston answered. 'The trouble is, they've got so many other commitments and the Army had first call on them. More often than not, the Tempest boys have got to go in alone, in which case their only chance of survival is to attack fast and low, right down on the deck, taking no evasive action at all. But you know all about that, of course.'

The two men talked for a while longer, discussing tactics and their mutual experiences. Later, after a wash and a short conference with his pilots, Yeoman made his way to the Intelligence Section — which was also in the mess annexe — to catch up on the latest situation reports and to study some photographs and data of some of the latest types of German aircraft, which had been encountered and sometimes shot down by Allied pilots in recent weeks.

The Intelligence Section appeared to have been a cloakroom of some sort, because there were rows of metal pegs along one of the walls. The other walls were covered with maps, silhouettes and photographs. Standing in front of one of the maps, two pilots from one of the Tempest squadrons were in deep conversation with a short, tubby squadron leader, whose balding head and thick-lensed spectacles gave him the air of a schoolmaster — which indeed he was, the war being some thing which he regarded as a temporary and annoying interruption of his true career, which was teaching modern languages to reluctant pupils at one of England's lesser public schools.

He looked around as Yeoman came into the room, gave a little embarrassed cough, and murmured 'Good evening, sir,' at the same time removing his glasses and polishing them on his sleeve.

Yeoman gave a sudden whoop of delight that startled the Tempest pilots, who looked at him in astonishment.

'Freddie Barnes! What the blazes are JAM doing here?' He strode forward and, seizing the Intelligence Officer's hand, pumped it vigorously, covering the older man in even more confusion.

'I, er ... I fell on hard times, sir.'

Yeoman laughed. 'Well, Freddie, I see that the hard times led to your promotion, so things can't be all that bad. My name's Yeoman, by the way,' he added, turning to the two pilots. 'Squadron Leader Barnes and I are old friends.'

'Didn't know he had any,' chuckled one of the the men. Yeoman looked at him, smiling.

'Well,' he said, 'I'll tell you this much. Freddie was my Intelligence Officer when I commanded 380 Squadron, flying Mosquitos, and he never once gave us any duff gen. He knows the Huns and their ways inside out.'

He looked at Barnes with great affection. 'It's good to see you, Freddie. We've got a lot of news to catch up on, but that can come later, over a beer or two. What I want to do now is have a look at the latest situation reports, and then you can tell me all about these new Hun kites our chaps have been meeting.'

Barnes handed him a pink folder and he leafed through its contents quickly, glancing at one of the wall maps from time to time to check the odd piece of information. On the map, Barnes or one of his few staff had already marked in the extent of the latest Allied advances on both eastern and western fronts; newly-captured airfields in 2nd Tactical Air Force's sector were circled in red, and by now there were quite a number.

Things were moving quickly now, towards the inevitable end. In the north, the British Second Army under Field Marshal Montgomery had captured Celle, thirty miles north-east of Hanover, cutting the road to Hamburg; on the morning of 12 April 'Monty's' tanks had plunged forward fifty-seven miles to reach the River Elbe. Also on the twelfth, elements of the United States Ninth Army had crossed the Elbe to capture the historic town of Brunswick, while in another dramatic armoured dash General Patton's Third Army had leaped forty-five miles across the River Saale to a point only forty miles from the Czech border.

In the south, the us Seventh Army captured Schweinfurt and Heilbronn, while the Fighting French took Baden Baden.

In the east, Vienna had fallen to the advancing troops of the Red Army, whose massive forces were now assembling for the final bloody assault on Berlin. Only a hundred miles separated the jaws of the giant nutcracker that was relentlessly squeezing Nazi Germany to extinction.

Yeoman gave the folder back to Barnes and then turned to the Intelligence reports on the latest types of enemy aircraft. Apart from technical data on estimated performances and so on, there were a lot of photographs — all 'stills' from gun-camera films exposed by Allied pilots — and some sketches, compiled by RAF intelligence staff from eye-witness accounts.

The first photograph Yeoman picked up showed a weird-looking contraption — a combination of two aircraft, one mounted on top of the other in pick-a-back fashion. It stirred a chord in Yeoman's memory and he showed it to Barnes, asking if there were any details.

The Intelligence Officer nodded. 'Oh, yes. It's what the Germans call "Mistel" — Mistletoe. The bottom aircraft, a Junkers 88 in this case, is filled with explosives and is steered towards its target by the upper aircraft, which can be either a Messerschmitt 109 or a Focke-Wulf 190. Our chaps have shot a few down lately.'

'I remember now,' Yeoman said. 'It was when we were flying air cover over the Normandy beaches in our Mosquitos just after the D-Day landings. Yves Romilly caught one and shot it down and nearly blew himself up when the thing exploded.' Romilly, a pilot in the Free French Air Force, had been one of Yeoman's flight commanders in No. 380 Squadron a year earlier. He asked Barnes if the latter had any news of him.

'The last I heard,' the Intelligence Officer told him, 'he was flying a desk in Paris, after the French had him transferred from the RAF. He was feeling very unhappy and doing his best to get back on operations.'

Yeoman grunted. He recalled how Romilly, soon after the capture of Paris, had visited his home capital for the first time in more than four years and had returned to the squadron thoroughly disillusioned with the attitude of many of his fellow countrymen, who were interested only in politics and who seemed to care nothing for the Frenchman who had fought and died and upheld the honour of France since the dark days of

1940. Perhaps, he thought, he could do something to help Romilly in his present predicament; at any rate, he resolved to try. He was surprised that the RAF had let the Frenchman go so easily in the first place, in view of Romilly's excellent record.

He turned back to the photographs, studying each one carefully. There were some good shots of the Me 262 jet, and an intriguing, rather blurred picture of a small jet aircraft with twin tail fins and its engine mounted in a pod on top of the fuselage, just behind the cockpit; this bore the caption 'Heinkel He 162', but there were no further details about it. Another hazy shot, which seemed to have been taken in the half-light, showed an even more curious machine. The photograph was supported by a rough sketch depicting an aircraft with a long, slender fuselage, straight wings and a cruciform tail unit, but the unusual point was that it had two engines — one in the nose and the other, a 'pusher' type, in the tail. The brief report attached to the sketch stated:

'Enemy aircraft encountered by Tempest of No. 3 Squadron over Bergedorf at 1820 hours on 2 April 1945. E/A showed no sign of jet propulsion, but escaped at 500 plus mph. Type unknown, but may be identical with new fighter type bearing enemy designation Dornier Do 335.'

Then there was another new type, a twin-engined jet bomber known as the Arado 234. It had, the report said, been used operationally in small numbers since the late summer of 1944. There was a full description of this machine, because an example had been captured intact when, hit by anti-aircraft fire during an attack on the Rhine bridge at Remagen in March, its pilot made a forced landing in a nearby field.

It did not need an expert to realize the astonishing technical progress made by Germany's aeronautical designers in bringing these radical new types into production; nor did it need an expert to predict that they had come too late to alter the course of the air war — although Yeoman shuddered to think what might have happened had they been available in sufficient numbers a year or so earlier. As it was, the brunt of the air fighting was still borne by two venerable piston-engined types, the Messerschmitt 109 and the Focke-Wulfe 190, which by 1945 had been stretched to the limit of their development. Astonishingly, the enemy still seemed to have plenty of fighters; but how they were still managing to produce them and keep them operating under appallingly adverse conditions was still something of a mystery.

Yeoman had made up his mind to make a tour of the airfield, but a glance outside told him that it would soon be dark and so, bearing in mind the cautions about booby traps and 'Werewolves' — fanatical Nazi civilians who were supposed to be lying in wait around every corner, ready to take pot-shots at any Allied personnel they saw wandering around — he decided that the tour could wait until the following morning and, accompanied by Freddie Barnes, he made his way to the dining room, where he found his pilots in animated conversation over platefuls of sausages, mashed potatoes and tinned tomatoes. They had also discovered several bottles of wine, which they were in the process of demolishing.

Yeoman and Barnes sat down opposite a ruddy-faced, brown-haired pilot who wore a squadron leader's rank badges and whose twinkling blue eyes belied the hard exterior lent to him by a broken nose and cauliflower ears, the relics of one of his main passions in life: amateur boxing. Tim Phelan had been 505 Squadron's commanding officer in the days when the unit flew Spitfires and Tempests, but when it had become the third RAF squadron to receive the new jet fighters and a wing commander — Yeoman — had been appointed to lead it, Phelan had turned down the chance of another command elsewhere and had happily stayed on as Yeoman's deputy.

Yeoman introduced Barnes to Phelan, and the latter filled a couple of glasses with wine and pushed them across the table. Barnes took a sip and made appreciative noises.

'Not bad,' he murmured in his mild fashion. 'Not bad at all. Johannesberger Kochsberg, I see, from the cellars of G.H. von Mumm. 1938 vintage, I'd say. That was a good year.'

'You can say that again,' Phelan grunted. 'We weren't fighting a war, for a start.'

'He means the wine, Tim,' Yeoman grinned. 'It's easy to tell you're no connoisseur. But then, neither am I, so we'll have to take Freddie's word for it. He's usually right.' The intelligence officer blushed and chewed furiously on a sausage.

'Have you had a look around yet, Tim?' Yeoman wanted to know. The Irishman nodded, and gave a sudden chuckle.

'I bumped into an amazing old codger just before I came into dinner, as I was walking down from my room. He was one of the Jerry civilians our people have kept on to do the cleaning up — a chap in his seventies, I'd say, with a great big bristling white moustache. He didn't seem to give a damn about being in an occupied country — in fact, I thought he seemed quite pleased to see us here. Anyway, he stopped me in the corridor and started hopping from one foot to the other, so I couldn't get past, all the time jabbing me in the chest with his finger and repeating: "*Var ofer! Var ofer — gut!*" I realized he was trying to tell me, in his broken English, that the war was over, so I started nodding like a lunatic. At that, he beamed all over his face, and said: "*Ja — var ofer, gut!* Now togedder ve go fight de Russkis, yes!" '

Those in earshot around the table roared with laughter at Phelan's story. Then Yeoman, suddenly serious, commented:

'I wonder if that's what they really think? Do they really believe that we'll sign an armistice here, in the west, so that they can transfer all the troops they have left to the eastern front, against the Russians?'

Phelan shrugged. 'Haven't the foggiest,' he said. 'Anything's possible; the Huns are a pretty weird bunch. Damned if I know what makes 'em tick.'

They were still discussing the German mentality when a young pilot came in, accompanied by an army liaison officer — a major -and the two sat down at Yeoman's table. The pilot explained that he was with a communications squadron and that he had been flying the army officer back to the United Kingdom from Celle when their aircraft had developed engine trouble, so he had made an emergency landing at Rheine. Mechanics were sorting the problem out, so he hoped to be on his way before long.

Covertly, Yeoman surveyed the major. The man looked tired and ill, and after a half-hearted attack on his food he pushed the plate aside and sat staring into space, a mug of tea in his hands. Eventually, Yeoman leaned over and tapped him on the arm.

'Are you all right, old boy?' he asked solicitously.

The Major started, looked at Yeoman as though he was seeing him for the first time, then smiled thinly, brushing a hand over his eyes.

'Sorry,' he apologized. 'I've had a hell of a day. I've been to Belsen, you see; we've arranged a truce with the Huns so that we can take the place over. We don't want the prisoners to get out, or we'll have typhus and God knows what else spreading all over the countryside.'

Yeoman was puzzled. 'Belsen? Where's that? And what's this about typhus?

The army officer blinked, then said: 'No, I don't suppose you've heard about Belsen yet. Well, let me tell you about it, and let me remind you that I've been there, and that I've seen it all for myself.'

He lit a cigarette with hands that trembled slightly, and Yeoman had not the heart to tell him that there was a 'no smoking' rule in the dining rooms of RAF messes. Instead, he quietly pushed a saucer across the table, for use as an ashtray.

'Belsen,' the major continued, 'or Bergen-Belsen, to give it its full title, is a place a few miles to the north of Celle. It is a concentration camp ... ' Around the table they listened in silence, unable even to begin to comprehend the horror that lay behind the officer's flat, toneless sentences, some frankly disbelieving even though inside them they knew the story was true. And who could blame them? How could these young men, hardened though they were by the deadly cut-and-thrust of air combat, even begin to visualize the stinking wooden huts where the wrecks of human beings — thousand upon thousand of them — lay on straw palliasses, the more fortunate covered with filthy blankets, so emaciated that at first glance it was impossible to tell whether they were male or female, their heads shorn, the agony of their suffering showing clearly in their expression, with eyes sunken and listless, cheek-bones prominent, too weak even to close their mouths? How could they begin to imagine the awful stench, so appalling that hardened British soldiers, no strangers to the smell of death, vomited continually when it assailed their nostrils? How could they hear the terrible, wailing cry — '*Essen* ... *essen* ... eat, eat' — that greeted the camp's liberators, or see through someone else's eyes the millions of bloated flies that covered the bodies of the dead, lying in mounds beside open graves? And the gas chambers ... and the crematoria ...

The catalogue of horror went on and on, as though the army officer was purging his soul of hideous memories. When his voice finally died away a terrible silence fell on the table. They had all heard of the Nazi concentration camps, of course, but none of them in his most awful nightmare had dreamed that they could be like this.

It was Tim Phelan who summed up the feelings of all of them.

'I hope that when they hang the bastards responsible for this, they die slowly!'

They got up and made their way to the bar, as though intent on washing a sudden filthy taste from their mouths. Freddie Barnes made his excuses and returned to his office. He had a top priority telephone call to make. It concerned Belsen; it also concerned Wing Commander George Yeoman, and part of his past.

Chapter Three

ORDER OF THE DAY: 16 APRIL 1945

Soldiers of the German front in the east!

The hordes of our Judeo-Bolshevist foe have rallied for the last assault. They want to destroy Germany and to extinguish our people. You, soldiers of the east, have seen with your own eyes what fate awaits German women and children: the aged, the men, the infants, are murdered, the German women and girls defiled and made into barrack whores. The rest are marched to Siberia.

We have been waiting for this assault. Since January every step has been taken to raise a strong eastern front. Colossal artillery forces are welcoming the enemy. Countless new units are replacing our losses. Troops of every kind hold our front.

Once again, Bolshevism will suffer Asia's old fate — it will founder on the capital of the German Reich.

He who at this moment does not do his duty is a traitor to the German nation. The regiments or divisions that relinquish their posts are acting so disgracefully that they must hang their heads in shame before the women and children who here in our cities are braving the terror bombing. If during these next days and weeks every soldier in the east does his duty, Asia's final onslaught will come to naught-just as the invasion of our Western enemies will in the end fail.

Berlin stays German. Vienna will be German again. And Europe will never be Russian!

Rise up to defend your homes, your women, your children — rise up to defend your own future!

At this hour the eyes of the German nation are upon you, you, my fighters in the east, hoping that your steadfastness, your ardour and your arms will smother the Bolshevist attack in a sea of blood!

This moment, which has removed from the face of the earth the greatest war criminal of all ages, will decide the turn of the fortunes of war!

ADOLF HITLER

Richter looked again at the last paragraph of the Order of the Day — which, although they did not know it then, would be Hitler's last — and a puzzled frown wrinkled his brow.

'What does he mean, "the greatest war criminal of all ages"? Who's he talking about?'

'He must mean Roosevelt,' von Gleiwitz told him. 'Roosevelt's dead, you know.'

His companion crumpled up the piece of paper and tossed it contemptuously aside.

'Load of bullshit,' he snorted. Von Gleiwitz looked around apprehensively. It was still dangerous to say such things — perhaps more so now than ever before — and Richter was far too outspoken for his own good. It was nothing short of a miracle how he had got away with it so far.

The two men were standing in the shelter of the trees in the middle of a pine forest that lay just to the east of Fürstenwalde. The autobahn that bisected the forest, a great, arrow-straight ribbon of concrete, ran from the southern outskirts of Berlin to Frankfurt-an-der-Oder, less than twenty-five miles away. The part beside which Richter and von Gleiwitz now stood was two thousand metres long, and was one of the two or three stretches of this size left intact in this area of Germany.

Behind the two men, in clearings hewn from the forest and connected to the autobahn by hastily-laid taxiways of steel mesh, the surviving Messerschmitt 262s of Jagdgeschwader 66 were being fuelled and armed for a sortie. There were only five of them now, for the other four had had to be left behind at Brandenburg through shortage of fuel when the order had come to fly east twenty-four hours earlier.

From that direction, borne on a chill breeze, came the sound of a terrific artillery bombardment. It had been going on since before dawn, and both pilots knew what it signified: the Russians were attacking in strength across the River Oder, in a last great drive that was designed to take them to the gates of Berlin.

For this offensive, the two Soviet Marshals Zhukov and Koniev had assembled a massive force of over one and a half million men, supported by 41,000 guns and 6,300 tanks, along the lines of the rivers Oder and Neisse, while on the captured airfields immediately to the east of these rivers the 1st, 8th and 16th Air Armies under Generals Krasovsky, Khryukin and Rudyenko had 8,400 combat aircraft at their disposal. At daybreak on this April Monday, the three Air Force Generals had launched the whole of their available bomber strength in a massive air onslaught against the German positions west of the two rivers. For hours, successive waves of bombers and fighter-bombers with strong fighter escort had roved almost at will over enemy territory, diving down to attack anything that moved. The few German fighters that tried to intervene were massacred. Then, in the wake of a huge artillery barrage, masses of Soviet shock troops had moved forward to storm the first line of German defences.

Richter had no real idea what was going on, because communications had broken down almost completely. His last instruction, received shortly after dawn, had been to take off with all available aircraft and bomb enemy bridgeheads in the Küstrin Kietz area. Whoever issued the order had apparently been unaware of the fact that JG 66's Me 262s were part of the last batch to come off the production line and had never been modified to carry bombs; nevertheless, Richter had decided to go ahead with the mission, his pilots attacking whatever they could find with cannon fire.

A heavy ground-fog had prevented an early -take-off, but now, at nine-thirty, it had dispersed sufficiently and Richter and his adjutant were taking a last look at the visibility along the autobahn. Satisfied that it was adequate they turned and walked back towards their aircraft. Neither man showed an inclination to hurry; they walked slowly along beside the taxi strip, their footfalls masked by the forest mould, savouring the mingled scents of resin and pine needles.

Fifteen minutes later they were strapped in their cockpits, nosing slowly out through the trees towards the autobahn, the hitherto peaceful forest made hideous by the shriek of the 262s' turbines. Sudden sunlight poured into Richter's cockpit as he swung off the metal strip and on to the long ribbon of concrete, a manoeuvre assisted as usual by his faithful mechanics.

The sun was in his eyes, blinding him, and he lowered his smoked goggles as he ran the 262's engines up to full power against the brakes. Then he was leaping forward, surging along the autobahn, the stately lines of trees streaming past his wingtips, conscious that if one of his turbojets lost even a fraction of power at this point he would veer to one side and bore a hole a hundred yards deep into the forest, ending his days in a tangle of metal and a hell of exploding fuel tanks.

But the engines responded beautifully and the 262 soared from the autobahn like a bird when he eased back the control column, the treetops falling away beneath him as he turned in a leisurely circle over the forest to let the others catch up with him. As he turned, he saw a great pall of smoke spreading out over the western horizon from the fires of Berlin, hammered incessantly now by British, American and Soviet bombers.

One by one the other four — von Gleiwitz, Dauer, Herold and Rothenberg — joined up with him and the 262s turned eastwards in a loose crescent-shaped formation, sweeping across the forest at a height of less than four hundred metres. As they thundered on, Richter noticed that the glare of the sun was growing dimmer, and when he raised his goggles he saw why; a haze of smoke was rising all along the eastern horizon too, masking the light and turning the bright morning sun into a dull red ball.

The five 262s whistled on over roads congested with troops and equipment moving east and where a steady flow of refugees headed west. In minutes, the broad metallic ribbon of the Oder appeared out of the smoke and haze and Richter brought the jets round in a left-handed turn towards their objective, the bridge across the river a kilometre or so east of Küstrin.-As they drew closer, Richter saw that the main bridge had been blown, but the Russians appeared to have thrown up pontoons. To judge from the smoke and flames and the flash of explosions, it appeared that the enemy must have already established a considerable foothold on the left bank of the river.

On his orders, the five jets slipped into line astern and plummeted down on the target at 800 km/h, diving through a fearsome barrage of light anti-aircraft fire. Their sheer speed, confusing the gunners, carried them through the worst of it, but the speed in itself gave the pilots little time to select their targets carefully. Richter opened fire at extreme range, concentrating on a cluster of tanks churning their way up from the river bank, and kept the triggers depressed until he was almost on top of them, seeing his exploding shells hurl up minor storms of dust and smoke. The shells made no impression on the heavily-armoured T-34s, bouncing off their steel hulls in sparkling flashes of light, but a group of infantry in Richter's line of fire went down like scythed grass. Then he was over and away, pulling hard on the stick and rocketing up almost vertically, with the flak baying ineffectually after him.

The other 262s completed their attacks without suffering damage and climbed after him, popping out of the smoke like glittering arrows. As they did so, Dauer's urgent voice came over the radio:

'Elbe Leader, look out, large bunch of Ivans to your left!'

Richter saw them at once: a big, unwieldy gaggle of Russian fighters, looking for all the world like a great flock of starlings wheeling over the stubble of a cornfield on an autumn day. There must have been nearly a hundred of them, diving down in sections from time to time to strafe some unseen target on the ground — probably German reinforcements, hastening to counter-attack the Russian bridgehead.

Quickly, Richter radioed his pilots and asked them if they had any ammunition left; all of them replied in the affirmative. Their commander assessed the situation in a moment or two. The 262s were now several thousand feet higher than the enemy fighters, and with their superior speed the jets stood a good chance of making one fast attack before getting away.

Richter knew that they might not be able to inflict much damage, but anything was worth a try if it brought some help to those poor devils on the ground.

'All right,' Richter called. 'Line abreast and straight through the middle of them, then down on the deck and head for home!'

The five jets fanned out and swept down on the Russians like a whirlwind, black trails streaming from their turbines as the pilots opened the throttles. The Russians, intent on shooting up targets on the ground, did not seem to be aware of the peril.

It was the first time Richter had encountered Soviet fighters since 1941, when as a lieutenant with the Jagdgeschwader he had later risen to command he had taken part in Operation Barbarossa, the German invasion of Russia. During the months that followed he had destroyed over forty Soviet aircraft, elevating himself to the ranks of Germany's leading aces. Now there was a chance — perhaps his last — to add to the score, although it no longer really mattered. For Germany, it was too late; nothing could halt the Red flood-tide now.

A Yakovlev Yak-3 fighter, camouflaged a drab khaki, danced briefly in his gunsight like a stiff-winged brown moth. He depressed the trigger for a second and the Yak-3's image disintegrated, ripped apart by the impact of the 30-mm shells. A severed wing whirled past, dangerously close, and Richter steered the 262 slap through the middle of the spreading smoke cloud of the explosion, ignoring the danger of debris entering the intakes of the turbines.

He snapped off a shot at a second fighter, missed, and held the 262 in its shallow dive, allowing the speed to build up before levelling out gently and heading west at maximum throttle, followed by the others. Behind them, the Russian fighters, milling around like a cloud of angry hornets, dwindled into the distance.

One by one, Richter's pilots called in. Dauer radioed that he too had shot down a Yak, while Herold had hit one but could not be certain of its fate. Von Gleiwitz, in disgust, reported that his cannon had jammed at the crucial moment.

There was no call from Rothenberg. Looking round, Richter saw that the fifth Me 262 was lagging badly behind, and asked its pilot if anything was wrong.

After a moment's delay, Rothenberg's voice came over the R/T. It was high-pitched, as though on the edge of panic.

'Elbe Leader, I am having trouble with the port turbine ... I think I may have been hit. The engine is not responding, and the temperature is going off the clock.'

Richter throttled back a little, allowing his fighter to drop astern of the rest while Rothenberg caught up with him. Carefully, he surveyed the other's aircraft.

'Listen, Hubert, there are no signs of damage or smoke, and that's a good sign. We are only a couple of minutes from home, so you go straight in to land. Can you hold on?'

'Yes, Leader, I ... I think so.'

Rothenberg's voice was trembling, and Richter felt a wave of sympathy for the boy. He knew only too well what it was like to nurse an ailing aircraft back to base, coaxing the last few miles out of it, the sweat pouring into your eyes and fear knotting your guts into an icy ball with the knowledge that you were too low to bale out if things went badly wrong ... and with the Messerschmitt 262, horribly unstable when flying on one engine, matters were even more complicated.

The other 262s still had a margin of fuel left, so Richter ordered them to circle over the pine forest while Rothenberg made his approach to land.

Richter looked down anxiously, his eyes following the glittering arrowhead that was Rothenberg's fighter. Its approach was perfectly straight, accurately lined up with the autobahn. With one turbine dead, the pilot must be exerting considerable strength to keep the fighter tracking on down towards the landing point.

Mentally, Richter gave Rothenberg full marks for his flying skill — and in that same instant, he realized with horror that the other pilot was too low. He opened his mouth to shout a warning over the radio, but he was too late.

Black smoke poured from the starboard engine of Rothenberg's 262 as the pilot, realizing his error, pushed open the throttle in a desperate attempt to gain some height. With the jet fighter in an assymetric condition, flying on one engine, it was exactly the wrong thing to do.

Helplessly, Richter watched as the 262 lifted a few hundred feet, rolling over on its back. Its undersurfaces caught the sunlight as it described a graceful parabola through the air. Then, still on its back, it nosed down and disappeared among the trees a couple of hundred metres to the left of the autobahn.

A vivid bubble of flame burst out above the treetops and a dense column of black smoke shot up, hanging poised for a few moments, as solid and motionless as a tombstone, before its top began to drift on the breeze.

Wordlessly, Richter led the other pilots down to land, the fighters rolling through the pall of oily smoke that now hung over the forest like a shroud.

The following morning, a Russian reconnaissance aircraft appeared over the pine forest, circling lazily and quartering the ground like a hawk. Against orders, a 20-mm flak battery opened up on it; the aircraft sheered away and disappeared in a shallow dive towards the east.

Furious, Richter placed the commander of the flak battery under arrest, court-martialled him half an hour later, and had him shot. It was the first time he had ever found it necessary to take such drastic action against anyone, and the incident upset him deeply, but he knew all too well what the consequences of the man's disobeyal of orders would be. With the grim certainty of what was to follow, he ordered his men to ensure that the camouflage of all equipment in the forest was as perfect as possible, and then to remain close to their dug-out shelters in anticipation of a major air attack.

It came just before noon. A hundred Soviet bombers came droning in from the east, with twice as many fighter escorts weaving protectively overhead. The Russian pilots knew exactly where to look. Taking the stretch of autobahn as their aiming point, they released their sticks of bombs in successive waves, carpeting the road and the forest on either side with explosions. Incendiaries set fire to the trees so that rivers of flame licked through the forest, seeking out fuel and ammunition dumps. Now that there was no longer any point in concealment, the crews of the flak batteries sited in the forest clearings put up a terrific barrage and several Russian aircraft fell burning from the sky, but in the end the encroaching flames forced the soldiers to abandon their guns and flee to safety, their uniforms scorched, choking in the dense smoke.

Richter and his pilots, together with their ground crews and the other personnel, cowered in slit trenches for twenty minutes while the attack continued without pause. As the bombers droned away, their fighter escorts swooped down and hosed the burning forest with cannon and machine-gun fire before turning away in the direction of the Oder.

As the last of the raiders flew away, Richter and von Gleiwitz stumbled out of the burning trees on to the shattered, bomb-cratered autobahn and tried to direct fire-fighting operations, but it was hopeless. The blaze was too big, the fire-fighting equipment too inadequate to cope with it. Besides, the precious Me 262s and all their stores and fuel had gone up in smoke; there was no point in staying.

A grim, black-faced Richter called his officers together and held a hurried council of war, the proceeding punctuated by frequent explosions as delayed-action bombs went off somewhere among the trees. There was nothing for it, Richter decided, but to scrape together all the transport that had survived the attack and head back towards Berlin. Perhaps, on one of the airfields near the capital, they could find more aircraft with which to carry on the fight, although Richter doubted it. He was aware that at least two-thirds of the Luftwaffe's surviving fighters in the Berlin sector had already flown south, where there was a plan to concentrate them for a 'last stand' in the Munich area.

Richter permitted himself a sardonic smile. To control this crazy 'last ditch' effort, a new Luftwaffe HQ had been set up just outside Munich — in a lunatic asylum.

It was late afternoon before the battered remnants of Jagdgeschwader 66 set off westwards along the autobahn, the few surviving vehicles overflowing with men. Fortunately, before leaving Brandenburg, Richter had had the foresight to secure written orders, signed by the C-in-C Luftwaffe, authorizing his unit to move to new locations 'as dictated by prevailing circumstances'; had he not possessed such orders, he would have undoubtedly had trouble with the 'head-hunters', the grim-faced field security police who were in position at every road junction, machine-pistols ready to shoot without question anyone even remotely suspected of deserting his post.

Germany in April 1945 was crawling with fear. It was reflected in the drawn faces of the batches of conscripts, the scrapings of the barrel, many of them men in their fifties or mere children of fifteen, as they trudged dejectedly eastwards like mindless sacrifices to some modern Moloch, whose terrible fires were now raging along a two-hundred mile stretch of the Oder; and it hung like a cloud over the hapless refugees who streamed in the other direction, men, women and children, the latter too exhausted and hungry even to cry.

Dear God, thought Richter, as the truck in which he rode nosed its way through the throng, its driver blowing his horn furiously and swearing at soldiers and civilians alike through the open window: dear God, how many times have I witnessed this spectacle before, in France, in Greece and in Russia! And now the roads of Germany are clogged with German civilians, blind with fear and panic, fleeing they know not where before the terror in the east, paying the price of a madman's ambition.

But five years earlier, none of them had believed that Hitler was a madman, and all of them had applauded his attempts to expand the frontiers of the Reich.

They were all guilty. This generation of Germans would always be guilty, its sleepless, guilt-laden ghosts doomed to wander on and on down the rivers of time, forever ...

Richter came fully awake with a start, suddenly realizing that he had been falling into a doze, his mind drifting with weariness. He passed a hand over his eyes and smiled weakly at von Gleiwitz, who sat beside him in the cab of the truck, sandwiched between himself and the driver. 'I think I'm beginning to feel the strain, Hasso,' he said. 'Somehow, everything seems unreal. I can't help imagining that we're all about to wake up from a nightmare.'

'It's real enough,' von Gleiwitz replied grimly, pointing ahead through the windscreen of the truck. 'Look.'

From horizon to horizon, a wall of smoke rose into the early evening sky. Beneath it lay Berlin, bombed by the British and Americans no fewer than eighty-five times since the beginning of February. For the Berliners, there was no respite; every night, following the American daylight bombers, squadrons of fast RAF Mosquitos would rove over the dying city, unloading their bombs into the inferno below.

The Germans were preparing, belatedly, to turn their capital into a fortified city. As Richter's small convoy rolled slowly on into Berlin's outer suburbs, it passed huge gangs of prisoners-of-war, mostly Russians in filthy brown rags, toiling side by side with slave labourers to build anti-tank ditches and other obstacles, always under the watchful and murderous eyes of their ss guards. Prisoners lay where they had collapsed from exhaustion; if rifle butts and kicks could not rouse them, they were despatched by a shot through the head.

In October 1943 SS Reichsführer Heinrich Himmler had stated: 'What happens to a Russian, or to a Czech, does not interest me in the slightest. What the nations can offer in the way of good blood of our type we will take, if necessary by kidnapping their children and raising them here with us. Whether nations live in prosperity or starve to death interests me only in so far as we need them as slaves for our Kultur: otherwise, it is of no interest to me. Whether ten thousand Russian females fall down from exhaustion while digging an anti-tank ditch interests me only in so far as the anti-tank ditch for Germany is finished.'

'Guilty,' Richter murmured again, half to himself, as the truck passed a heap of ragged bodies dumped carelessly by the roadside, Von Gleiwitz looked sideways at him and made no comment.

Negotiating the rubble-filled streets of Berlin took three hours, and it was dark before the convoy reached its destination, the Luftwaffe HQ compound at Wildpark-Werder. Richter ordered his men to remain where they were and, together with von Gleiwitz, went into the building, both men showing their identity documents to the bored-looking sentries at the door.

Inside the headquarters, chaos reigned supreme, and Richter quickly discovered that no one was interested in the present plight of Jagdgeschwader 66, a fighter unit without aircraft. In the end, after kicking his heels in various anterooms for the best part of two hours, Richter took the law into his own hands and, striding purposefully through echoing corridors to the inner sanctum of the HQ, burst into a room full of startled staff officers and demanded to see the commander-in-chief.

A hawk-faced colonel with iron-grey hair and a patch over his right eye looked up from a desk and grinned.

'So, Richter, it's you. Still the same young hothead as ever, I see.' He waved an imperious hand, silencing a red-faced staff major who had been about to protest at Richter's intrusion, and then fixed the latter with his single piercing eye.

'I know why you are here, Richter,' the colonel said. 'You have been destroyed as an effective fighting unit, and you are seeking further orders.' He spread his hands expressively. 'God only knows what we can do for you, but at least we can try. Now, what is the exact state of your men and equipment?'

Richter told him, more than a little embarrassed by the fact that he could not remember the other's name, although he had served briefly under him in Russia in the autumn of 1941. The colonel listened without interruption, nodding soberly from time to time, then rose and left the room, ordering the younger man to remain where he was. Richter put on his best granite face and spent the next few minutes glaring at the staff major, who kept glancing at the pilot's decorations and who finally buried his red, discomforted face inside a bulky dossier.

The colonel's countenance, when he returned, was grave. He explained that he had just been to see General Roller, Hermann Göring's chief of staff, in search of instructions, and that Koller had wordlessly shown him an order he had just received. It was signed by Adolf Hitler himself. The colonel handed a copy to Richter, who looked at the wording through eyes blurred with fatigue and read it twice before he grasped its simple and brutal meaning.

All Luftwaffe units which were no longer capable of participating in the air defence of the Reich were to be disbanded forthwith and their personnel assigned to the armies in the east.

Deep down inside him, Richter had expected something of the sort; nevertheless, it came as a profound shock to see the ultimate fate of the Jagdgeschwader he had commanded so proudly sealed in a couple of cold, short sentences. He only half heard the colonel explaining quietly that some thirty-five thousand Luftwaffe and Navy personnel had already been transferred to the east to reinforce the armies on the Oder-Neisse Line; the words did nothing to lessen the bitter blow.

Richter slept little that night; indeed, sleep would have proved impossible, even had he wished it, for the crowded, foul-smelling air raid shelter he shared with his men trembled all night to the concussion of exploding bombs and the salvoes of anti-aircraft batteries as Mosquitos droned overhead in an almost constant stream. So, weary as he was, Richter stayed awake, staring into the dimly-lit recesses of the shelter, but seeing instead a long procession of events and faces parade before him, like Macbeth's phantoms: re-living the great hunt across Russia in the latter half of 1941, when enemy aircraft fell in their hundreds before the Luftwaffe's guns, before Winter clamped its icy hand across Hitler's ambitions; winging once more over the green, stunted olive groves of Greece, and diving through the murderous flak over Malta; seeing, with enormous clarity, the faces of dear comrades, swallowed up in the Great Fighter Graveyard that western Europe became after the Allied landings in Normandy in 1944.

Men had come and gone, campaigns had come and gone, but the Jagdgeschwader, the old Fighting 66th, had soldiered on inviolate, its identity intact, until now. So here it was all to end, in the burning ruins of Berlin, the old dreams of glory gone forever.

But the pride would live on; the pride in having belonged. All those who had served with the 66th, and who survived these last bitter days, would carry that pride with them to the grave.

*

The men of JG 66 stood in close ranks, their backs ramrod-stiff, staring fixedly ahead of them. The morning was cold, with a stiff wind blowing from the north-east. The wind carried the dull thunder of artillery fire; it seemed to grow louder with every passing hour.

A small knot of officers stood out in front of the men, facing them. General Koller was there, and the one-eyed staff colonel, but it was on Richter that the attention of everyone was focused as the commander of JG 66 made the last address he would ever make to the men who had served him so well. It was a very short address, but it said all that Richter wished to say.

Hasso von Gleiwitz, standing in the parade adjutant's position, was not really listening, for his mind was already preoccupied with thoughts of the immediate future. He and Richter would both be remaining at Luftwaffe Headquarters on the orders of General Koller, although both had expressed a strong wish to go with their men, and von Gleiwitz's agile mind was already grappling with the problem of how to get himself and his commanding officer out of Berlin and away to the west before the city was surrounded by the Russians, as now seemed inevitable. Richter's speech came to him only in isolated fragments, punctuated by the distant crash of gunfire.

'Comrades ... a long and bitter fight ... upheld the honour of our Fatherland ... no shame ... undefeated in the air ... every one of your ... always part of the 66th, for you will never forget ... take courage, and do your duty ... '

Richter himself was aware how inadequate his words must seem, and yet they had an effect; tears were coursing unashamedly down the cheeks of some of the men, and not only those who had lengthy service with the Jagdgeschwader.

He had not prepared his address, and now he was running out of words. He had to say something quickly, something in conclusion that would leave an impact on the minds of his audience. Yet what could he say? What hope could he give these men, most of whom would probably be dead in a few days' time?

Suddenly, in a flash, he had it. It did not matter to him that any talk that even hinted at the possibility of Germany's defeat could still be punished by arrest and execution; only by looking beyond defeat could he give his men any kind of meaningful message. He drew himself up, and his voice rang out loud and vibrant.

'Comrades! Look forward to the future, beyond the hardship of the months ahead, to the day when the eagles of the 66th will fly again in a Germany reborn from these ashes! For I say to you that Germany *will* rise again, and on that day she will once more have need of her young eagles!'

It was enough, and Richter's words had clearly not displeased General Roller. Now, accompanied by von Gleiwitz, Richter moved among the ranks of men, shaking hands with each individual and wishing him luck. It saddened him to think that Dauer and Herold were going, too, but the two pilots had volunteered and no objection had been raised. At least their presence would help keep the morale of the men at a reasonable level.

Von Gleiwitz dismissed the parade and Richter stood there in the wind, watching the men as they moved off section by section towards the trucks that were standing ready to take them first to an army depot where they would be issued with rifles and equipment, and then towards whatever destiny awaited them in the fighting that raged along the Oder.

Richter turned and walked slowly back towards the headquarters building, wondering what possible use he could be now. The recollection of his fine words brought a cynical smile to his lips, for he himself had not believed them. Germany would never rise again; the Allies, and particularly the Russians, would make certain of that. They would crush her underfoot like a worm and grind her to extinction. She could expect no better treatment.

Chapter Four

FOR THE PILOTS OF NO. 505 SQUADRON, IT HAD BEEN A WEEK of intense frustration. Two or three times a day, pairs of Meteors had been sent out on patrol towards the north and east, where the British Second Army was driving on towards the north German ports, but they still had orders to remain well clear of the front line and no enemy aircraft had been sighted. To add to their bitterness, they knew that the Tempest squadrons of 122 Wing, with whom they shared Rheine, were finding and destroying many enemy machines in the course of their offensive patrols in the Hamburg, Lübeck and Bremen areas. What was even worse, moreover, was that two of the Meteor pilots had been shot at by uncomfortably accurate British anti-aircraft fire — and this during a sortie specially laid on to show the ack-ack gunners the difference between a Meteor and a Messerschmitt 262.

The general feeling was aptly summed up by Tim Phelan's remark, 'What the bloody hell was the use of sending us out here in the first place, if they won't let us get stuck in?' and the atmosphere of gloom and disillusionment was thick enough to be sliced with a knife when Yeoman walked into the Squadron's dispersal. A couple of grunts answered his 'Good morning, chaps', and the pilots failed to notice the fact that he was desperately trying to keep a straight face as he went over to the stove and poured himself a mug of tea from the urn that was burbling gently on top.

'It's Hitler's birthday today, so I'm told', he remarked casually. 'I've been thinking — maybe we ought to celebrate.'

A couple of faces turned towards him in curiosity and he pulled a slip of paper from his trouser pocket, studying it with mock intensity.

'I don't know if anybody's interested,' he said mildly, 'but it says here that No. 505 Squadron is released for offensive operations with effect from 0600 hours on Friday, the twentieth of April — '

There was more, but his words were drowned in the general pandemonium as the pilots clustered round him, all as jubilant now as schoolchildren and demanding to know what the first operation was to be. Tim Phelan slapped him on the back with a force that made his teeth rattle and grinned at him hugely.

'Well done, George! Now we can get at 'em, before it's too late!'

'Don't thank me,' Yeoman said. 'It was Group Captain Kingston who pulled it off — he must have pals in the Air Ministry. Anyway, let's get down to business.'

He produced a map and unfolded it, spreading it out on the floor and crouching down beside it. The others formed a half-circle behind him, peering over his shoulder to follow the movements of his finger as he pointed out the details of the coming mission.

'All right, first of all the general picture.' Yeoman's finger traced a line running roughly east-west across northern Germany.

'Here is the Second Army, pushing up towards Bremen on a fairly broad front, with two distinct prongs over on the right, here, driving northwards over the Lüneburg Heath towards Lübeck. A lot of weight is being put into this part of the offensive, because if our people reach Lübeck in time they will effectively trap the German forces in Denmark, forestalling any possible move to break out and perhaps rush to the help of their troops fighting east of Berlin. Also, our Intelligence people believe that the Huns are assembling a lot of shipping in these northern ports, with the idea of transferring large numbers of troops and supplies to Norway for a last-ditch stand there. So you see, it's vital for Second Army to reach the coast as soon as possible, and that means a correspondingly big effort on the part of 2nd Tactical Air Force.'

Yeoman's finger moved across the map, indicating three separate points.

'A lot of enemy forces,' he continued, 'are concentrated in the triangle formed by these three roads, here, with Hamburg, Lauenburg and Lübeck forming the points. Second Army's spearheads are here, on this side of the River Elbe just south of Lauenburg.

'Our orders, quite simply, are to create the maximum possible havoc within this triangle, to prevent the enemy forces from falling back on Lübeck in anything like reasonable order. So it's a ground attack sortie, and we're looking for enemy transport, especially of the soft-skinned variety. It won't be a picnic, because there'll be a lot of light flak, but we won't be on our own; some Typhoons are going in ahead of us to work the area over, and the Tempest boys will be flying top cover.'

Yeoman rose to his feet, wincing a little; his foot still troubled him from time to time.

'One more thing, before we get down to the finer details. I repeat that this is a ground attack sortie; we are to avoid combat with the Luftwaffe unless it proves impossible not to.'

A groan of disappointment was quickly stilled by Yeoman's upraised hand.

'Just a minute, before you all start moaning. It's just possible that if we do encounter the Luftwaffe, we might inadvertently manoeuvre ourselves so that they are between us and the Elbe-in which case we shall have to fight our way through them in order to get home. If you all follow my meaning.' Their broad grins assured him that they did.

Take-off was fixed for 0800. Twelve Meteors were detailed for the sortie; these were to be divided into two flights of six, with Yeoman leading one and Tim Phelan the other.

The pilots, completed their briefings, collected their helmets and parachutes and went out to their aircraft. After a word with his ground crew, Yeoman climbed into the narrow cockpit by way of the spring-loaded footsteps and handholds built into the fuselage sides and strapped himself in, adjusting the height of his seat slightly by operating the handle on its right-hand side.

Leaving the cockpit canopy open for the time being, he methodically worked his way through the cockpit checks, then told the ground crew to plug in the ground starter battery. A look around assured him that no persons or loose equipment were in the vicinity of the air intakes or the wake of the jet pipes, and he signalled that he was ready to start the engines.

Checking that the twin throttle levers were fully back and the high pressure and low pressure cocks both in the 'on' position, he switched on the low pressure pump of the port engine and then, when the fuel pressure warning light flicked out, he pressed the starter pushbutton for a couple of seconds.

A low whine quickly grew in volume as the engine, fed by electrical power from the ground starter battery, began to turn and accelerate steadily to between 5,000 and 6,000 rpm. The jet pipe temperature needle fluctuated a little, then settled down to just under 500 degrees centigrade, which was entirely satisfactory.

When both engines were running and the ground starter battery disconnected, Yeoman ensured that all warning lights were out and that the flaps were working properly. He switched on his radio compass and checked the setting of the direction indicator against it, then made a brief radio call to flying control to check the efficiency of his VHF set and also to obtain the latest altimeter settings.

One by one, the other pilots called in to say that their engines were running and that they were ready to go. Thankfully, there had been no 'wet starts', which sometimes occurred when the engines failed to light up and consequently became flooded with fuel; in that event, the pilot had to wait until all surplus fuel had drained from the engine nacelle and been removed from the jet pipe by the ground crew before going through the whole starting procedure again.

Yeoman gave the thumbs-up sign to the pilot of the number two Meteor — a tubby, cheerful young flying officer named Phil Trussler, whose three great loves in life were aircraft, fishing and tall women, in that order — and then cranked his cockpit hood closed, afterwards waving to the ground crew to remove the wheel chocks.

The Meteors taxied out towards the runway in pairs, each pilot testing the brakes after his aircraft had moved forward a few yards. Taxi-ing was accomplished by the co-ordinated use of throttles and brakes when turning, but the pilots had to be careful, for rapid opening and closing of the throttles could result in excessive jet pipe temperatures. Fuel consumption was also high during taxi-ing — over a gallon a minute for each engine at idling rpm. These, however, were the only drawbacks, for the Meteor's tricycle undercarriage made it a joy to handle on the ground and the visibility from the cockpit, set well forward, was excellent and a point over which to enthuse by pilots who had been used to tailwheel aircraft, their vision impeded by large, powerful piston engines in front of the cockpit which made it necessary to weave madly while taxi-ing in order to avoid running into something.

The leading pair of Meteors halted short of the runway and the pilots carried out their take-off checks. Yeoman always said these out loud; it was a habit he had acquired during his days as a trainee pilot, and it had stayed with him ever since.

'Trim: neutral. Fuel: contents okay, HP and LP cocks on, low pressure pumps on, ventral tank transfer control off, balance cock shut. Flaps:

one-third down, selector neutral. Pneumatic supply: at least two hundred pounds per square inch. Air brakes: closed. Hood: closed. Direction indicator: synchronized with radio compass and uncaged. Harness: adjusted and locked.'

Satisfied that all was well Yeoman turned his fighter on to the runway, with Trussler lining up alongside. The Tempests that were to take part in the operation had already taken off some minutes earlier; their much greater endurance would permit them to rove over the target area for some time before the Meteors arrived, drawing any hostile fighters on to themselves.

Yeoman, with Trussler duplicating his every movement, taxied forward a short distance to straighten the nosewheel, then opened both throttles smoothly to take-off rpm. There was no tendency for the Meteor to swing, because there was no large propeller trying to pull it off to one side, and it accelerated smoothly to 70 knots, at which point the pilot gently eased the control column back to lift the nosewheel just clear of the ground.

The acceleration was slow — much slower than with a piston-engined type — and the take-off was prolonged, the Meteor doing its best to hug the ground for as long as possible. Mindful that the aircraft was fully laden, with its ventral fuel tank attached, Yeoman held it with the nosewheel just off the ground until the airspeed indicator showed 110 knots, then literally pulled it clear of the runway with a sudden firm backward pressure on the stick. He waited until he was comfortably airborne, then applied the brakes to stop the wheels spinning before retracting the undercarriage.

He allowed the aircraft to accelerate to 155 knots before pulling up in a gentle climbing turn, circling the airfield while the other five pairs took off in succession and came up to join formation. Then, with everyone nicely in position, he led the twelve Meteors in a steady climb at 190 knots up to ten thousand feet, swinging round on to a compass heading of 065 degrees.

From a height of nearly two miles, there was nothing to show that war had so recently raged over northern Germany; the thickly-wooded countryside north-east of Rheine looked nothing but peaceful, its innumerable lakes and waterways gleaming in the thin morning sun. Only when the great sprawling industrial complex of Bremen came crawling over the far horizon, over on their left, did signs of bitter conflict become apparent — for Bremen, towards which General Dempsey's Second Army had launched an attack that morning, was in flames from end to end, dense smoke billowing up thousands of feet from countless fires started by Allied bombing and shellfire.

Yeoman gave a little involuntary shudder, recalling Bremen's formidable anti-aircraft defences, and was glad that he was not one of the tactical bomber pilots taking part in that final assault. In order to keep well clear of the front line at this point he brought the formation round in a detour to the south, crossing the River Weser near the town of Verden. The latter had been recently captured by the British, and was almost completely devastated; the Germans, Yeoman thought, were still capable of resisting with astonishing ferocity.

The twelve Meteors resumed their original course, crossing Lüneburg Heath on a north-easterly heading, and now Yeoman brought them down in a shallow descent as they approached the target area. So far, they had not seen any other aircraft, but now a cluster of black dots appeared up ahead, growing steadily larger, and Yeoman warned the other pilots to be on the alert and ready for a possible engagement.

The black dots, however, resolved themselves into Spitfires; they took no notice whatsoever of the Meteors, but passed quickly by to starboard at a lower altitude, heading towards Celle. From now on, however, the sky ahead seemed to be filled with aircraft, crossing and re-crossing the front line or circling over some distant target. All of them were identified as friendly.

The Meteors were now heading towards the northernmost tip of the Second Army's advance, to the north of Lüneburg. The old Hanseatic port of Hamburg, shattered and gutted by three years of almost constant air attack, an even greater inferno than Bremen, lay off their port wingtips, crouching as though for protection against the great swathe of the Elbe Estuary.

Yeoman pressed the R/T button.

'Ramrod Leader to Ramrod aircraft. Enemy territory ahead, on the other side of the Elbe. Keep your eyes peeled.'

He called up the Tempests but it was a while before he made contact, for they were sweeping the sky far ahead, over Lübeck, and at that moment were engaged in a stiff fight with some Focke-Wulf 190s.

On the other side of the river the landscape was dotted with fires. The pilots could clearly see shells bursting on the ground as the Second Army's artillery pounded enemy positions to the north-east of Laucnburg, but so far there was no flak.

Yeoman led the Meteors over Schwarzenbek, then swung left to intercept the Hamburg-Lübeck autobahn, which the Tempest leader had indicated to be crammed with enemy transport of all kinds. So it was, but two squadrons of Typhoons were already working it over very satisfactorily and so Yeoman turned his squadron north-eastwards again in the hope of finding some worthwhile targets close to Lübeck itself.

Lübeck-Blankensee airfield was dead ahead, but columns of smoke rising from it indicated that it had already been heavily attacked and Yeoman doubted that much of significance would be left; at any rate, it was not worth risking a low-level run through intense flak to find out.

He was beginning to despair of ever locating something to shoot at when Trussler's excited voice burst over the radio.

'Aircraft at two o'clock — on the lake!'

Yeoman looked ahead and to his left and picked out what Trussler had seen almost immediately. To the south of the airfield, a lake about four miles long by a mile wide ran through a wooded valley as far as the little town of Ratzeburg. At the northern end of the lake, a couple of miles from the airfield, six big flying-boats were moored, and some sort of boat traffic was going on between them and the shore. The aircraft were three-engined Dornier 24s. Yeoman guessed that they had only recently arrived, otherwise the fighter-bombers which had attacked the airfield must surely have spotted them.

'All right,' Yeoman ordered, 'get stuck in. Attack in pairs.'

He pushed forward the stick and went down in a long, shallow dive towards the target, with Trussler a few yards away from his wingtip. The two Meteors flattened out just over the surface of the water and sped up the lake at terrifying speed, the scream of their engines echoing from the low hills on either side.

Anti-aircraft fire lanced out at them, but it was only small-arms stuff and they ignored it. In any case, the tracers fell a long way behind the fleeting aircraft as the gunners hopelessly misjudged the Meteors' speed.

A Dornier, its fuselage and wings camouflaged in splinters of grey and dark blue, danced between the luminous triangles of Yeoman's gunsight.

He pressed the gun button and the Meteor shuddered as the four 20-mm cannon pumped their explosive shells towards the enemy aircraft. Fountains of spray erupted just short of the Dornier, then the shells 'walked' right across it in flashing explosions. There was a brilliant spurt of light as a fuel tank erupted, and fragments of burning wreckage spun off the Dornier to fall sizzling into the lake.

Yeoman streaked over the top of the burning wreck and pulled back the stick, taking the Meteor several thousand feet up in an arrowing climb before levelling out and coming round in a circle, looking down to see the results of the attack.

The other Meteors were flashing in pairs across the lake, making short work of the remaining Dorniers. By the time the last pair began their dive all six flying boats were on fire and sinking, so instead the two pilots strafed what appeared to be some army trucks grouped close to a jetty.

The two Meteors had barely cleared the target area safely when a terrific explosion enveloped the trucks and a huge fireball burgeoned up several hundred feet, spreading out into a cloud of brown and yellow smoke out of which white tendrils shot in all directions. At least one of the trucks must have been crammed with ammunition.

'Nice work, boys. Let's go home. Is everyone okay?'

One of the last pair of jets to attack had collected a single bullet in its port wing, but all the rest were unharmed. Yeoman hoped, now, that they would not encounter any opposition during the return flight, for their fuel was running low and there would be none to spare for combat. All in all, it had been a very good morning's work, and his one wish was to shepherd the squadron back to base without mishap.

He need not have worried. As the Meteors flew back towards Bremen, there was a momentary scare as a shoal of single-engined aircraft came slanting down out of the layer of wispy cloud that was beginning to spread across the sky, then relief as Yeoman identified the powerful, aggressive silhouettes of 122 Wing's Tempests.

They formed up on either side of the Meteors, waggling their wings, and with the sun at its back the whole formation set course south-westwards across the rolling plain of Lower Saxony.

Chapter Five

ON THE MORNING OF SATURDAY, 21 APRIL — THE DAY AFTER No. 505 squadron's jets carried out their first successful ground attack sortie — a twin-engined C47 transport aircraft of the USAAF landed at Rheine and whisked away Freddie Barnes, the Intelligence Officer, together with two colleagues from a similar branch of the army. Barnes apologized to Yeoman before his departure, saying that he was not allowed to say where he was going, or why, but that he would only be absent for a couple of days. Yeoman had shrugged understanding^, telling himself that 'spies', as the RAF nicknamed its intelligence personnel, were an odd lot and a law unto themselves at times.

The C-47, in fact, took Barnes and the other officers to the Paris airport of Le Bourget, and from there a staff car drove them to the Hotel Royal Monceau in the 14th arondissement. This hotel, in the spring of 1945, was well known to almost everyone in the French capital as the main United States Navy officers' billet; what was less well known, however, was that it was also a rendezvous for various sections of the Allied Intelligence Services.

It was here, behind locked doors, that a very secret scientific intelligence group known as Alsos directed operations throughout western Europe. The Greek word 'alsos' meant 'grove' and had been selected because the mastermind behind the enterprise was an American general named Leslie R. Groves. In just a few months time, the world would know more of General Groves, for he was the head of an ultrasecret research programme in the United States known as Project Manhattan. Its goal was the production of a weapon which, if it worked, would bring a speedy end to the war against Japan: the atomic bomb.

Squadron Leader Freddie Barnes had been part of the Alsos Mission since the autumn of 1944, having been selected because of his expertise in interrogating captured Luftwaffe officers. In the United States, where a prototype atomic bomb was still a long way off being tested, a B-29 Superfortress Group was already training to drop the operational version of such a weapon, and it was vital to know if there was any indication that a Luftwaffe bomber unit had been carrying out specialist training of a similar kind.

Right up to February 1945, Allied fears had been strong that German scientists might have succeeded in outstripping their American and British counterparts in atomic research to the point where they were capable of producing an operational bomb, but as the Alsos scientists pushed deeper into liberated Europe in the wake of the Allied advance such deep fears had gradually receded. As more documents on the enemy atomic research effort fell into Allied hands, it was becoming increasingly clear that although the Germans had perhaps enjoyed a slight lead as far back as 1942, their achievements after that had fallen a long way short of the level of Anglo-American research.

This was to become even more apparent at the meeting now attended in Paris by Barnes and some twenty other people, some civilian and some military, under the chairmanship of the eminent physicist Dr Samuel A. Goudsmit. After each member had given his individual report, Goudsmit gave a broad smile and informed them that the spearheads of the Alsos group, operating right up front with the Allied armies, had scored notable successes in different parts of Germany. He produced a note written by Colonel Boris T. Pash, a senior American intelligence officer who commanded the Alsos group accompanying the us 7th Army in its drive eastwards from Heidelberg, and read it out to the assembly.

'After three hours here (in the village of Stadtilm) it is obvious we have a gold mine. All the personnel who worked on the enemy atomic project, together with material, secret files etc., were carted away from here on Sunday by the Gestapo, destination unknown. However, we have Dr Berkei, who has been on the project from the beginning and who is telling all; sets of revealing files; parts of the U-Machine (uranium pile); much equipment, counters etc.

'I think you should get here post haste ... We will certainly learn the broad outlines of the whole project here and in the south fill in the technical details.'

Goudsmit also told them that Alsos teams in northern Germany, investigating the newly-captured town of Lindau, had seized another key scientist and a massive quantity of research files from the Reich Research Council, while a centrifuge laboratory had been found in a silk spinning mill at Celle. Most important of all, however, was the discovery near Stassfurt of 1,200 tons of uranium ore, mined in the Congo in the 1930s and stockpiled in Belgium; it had been seized by the German Army in 1940 and shipped to Germany, since when no more had been heard of it until now. It represented the bulk of uranium supplies in Europe, and its capture by the Allies seemed to remove definitely any possibility of the Germans making use of an atomic bomb.

After rounding up the current situation Goudsmit left the meeting to travel to Heidelberg, and his place in the chair was taken by a senior Royal Air Force officer, an air commodore named Sampson. Barnes had known Sampson for some time; the air commodore had been head of the British Air Ministry's Special Operations Directorate before becoming a key figure in the newly-created Anglo-American Nuclear Intelligence Committee in the autumn of 1944. Now, as he faced his audience, he was by no means as optimistic as Goudsmit had appeared.

'Gentlemen,' he began, 'let us not for one moment imagine that the recent good news about the extent of the enemy's atomic research, or lack of it, means that our task is coming to an end. On the contrary: it is only just beginning.'

He paused and looked searchingly at the faces round the table for a few moments, then continued:

'As hostilities in Europe draw to a close, our task assumes even more vital importance. We must ensure that we cast our net as widely as possible in order to capture every scientist of note, and every scrap of documentary evidence, concerned in or with the German atomic research programme. To put it bluntly, we must take all possible steps to ensure that no key enemy personnel fall into the wrong hands.'

Equally as bluntly, one of the civilians, a grey-haired American with a clipped moustache, asked:

'Does that mean Soviet hands?'

The air commodore nodded soberly. 'It does. As far as we know, the Russians do not have any kind of atomic research programme. However, we must not underestimate the expertise of their scientists; they are very quick to learn and to adapt their thinking to fall in with new methods. It would not take them long to realize the overwhelming potential of the research the Germans have been carrying out in parallel with ourselves if they were fortunate enough to capture even a small number of top enemy scientists.'

Sampson extracted a cigarette from a silver case, tapped it vigorously on the table, and held it unlit between his fingers while he looked at a folder on the table in front of him.

'In south and central Germany,' he went on, 'thanks to the speed of our advances, we have managed to overrun several atomic research centres before their personnel could escape. We have also had similar successes in the north, albeit to a lesser extent; fortunately, German scientific personnel in Berlin, which is now threatened with encirclement by the Russians, appear to have left the capital some months ago to continue their researches in quieter areas.'

He tapped the folder in front of him and finally applied a lighter to his cigarette.

'Here,' he said, 'we have a list of names of notable enemy scientists who have already fallen into our net, or who are likely to do so within the next few days. Six very important names, however, are missing, and now I am going to tell you why.'

There was complete silence in the room, apart from the muted rumble of the traffic on the roads that by-passed the Parc Monceau. Then Sampson began to tell them what he knew.

'Last autumn, through various channels, we established contact with a group of six enemy scientists who were involved in the German atomic research project, and who were seriously perturbed by the prospect of what might happen if Germany became the first to secure an operational atomic bomb. All the scientists, needless to say, were secretly opponents of the Nazi regime.

'We agreed to help them get out of Germany if they would subsequently tell us everything they knew about the atomic project, and word reached us that they had agreed to our terms. We therefore infiltrated two of our top Special Operations Executive agents into Germany — how we did it is of no importance-and they were to make contact with the scientists in Osnabrück, where the Germans were to be attending some sort of conference.'

The air commodore stubbed out his cigarette in a deliberate gesture.

'The contact was made, we know that, but someone must have talked. The next information we had was that the scientists and our two operatives were being held in a house on the outskirts of a village named Berge, about twenty-five miles from the Dutch border. The house was a headquarters of the Abwehr, which as you all know is the German Military Intelligence Service.

'We had to act quickly,' the air commodore continued, 'before our people and the scientists were handed over to the Gestapo. You know what their methods are like; our operatives might have held out for a long time under interrogation, but we felt sure that the scientists would have quickly broken under torture and told everything they knew, implicating God knows how many people who are going to be of enormous use to us alive after this war is over.

'We therefore ordered an air attack on the house by a squadron of Mosquitos, No. 380, which specialized in low-level bombing techniques. The crews were briefed by the officer seated at the far end of the table, Squadron Leader Barnes, who at that time was the Squadron's intelligence officer. Barnes?' Barnes cleared his throat and addressed the gathering, showing none of the signs of nervousness he customarily displayed when briefing aircrews for a mission.

'The attack was carried out late in September last year by ten Mosquitos, each carrying two 500-lb bombs. It was a complete success and the house was destroyed, although — ' he hesitated slightly, although, I might add, at considerable cost in aircraft and men.' The Intelligence Officer looked down at the table, fidgeting with his fingers.

'Yes,' Sampson continued, 'it was a costly attack. The man who led it, Squadron Leader Yeoman — who is now a wing commander, with a jet fighter squadron at Rheine — was quite rightly awarded the Distinguished Service Order for leading it.' A bitter note crept into the air commodore's voice.

'Unfortunately,' he went on, 'our intelligence turned out to have been less uP-to-date than we believed. After the attack, in which three of the scientists and one of the agents were killed, it was established that the Abwehr had already moved the other three scientists — top men, all of them — and the second agent to another location. After that, we lost track of them for something like four months, until we had further intelligence that all four were in a concentration camp — Belsen, to be precise.'

The air commodore lit another cigarette and leaned back in his chair, exhaling the smoke slowly through his nostrils, then quietly resumed his story.

'When British troops captured Belsen some days ago, an Alsos group visited the camp with the express mission of locating the scientists and the SOE operative. They failed to do so for the simple reason that the four prisoners were no longer there. It took us two days to establish, through interrogations of senior camp staff, that all four had succeeded in escaping about a fortnight earlier, apparently with outside help. It seems that their decision to try and escape must have been made following a rumour that all the inmates of the camp were to be exterminated before the place was captured by us.

'The point, gentlemen, is that only one anti-Nazi resistance organization is powerful enough, and efficient enough, to help anyone escape from such a well-guarded place as a concentration camp.'

'The communists,' the man with the clipped moustache murmured.

'Exactly. We don't know how they did it, but the facts are there. And if the communists really were the masterminds behind the escape, it is highly unlikely that the scientists and our agent will be heading in any direction other than east. Our guess, in fact, is that they are in hiding in Berlin, waiting for the arrival of the Russians ... assuming, of course, that they are still alive. There is always a chance that they may not be.'

'Who exactly are the scientists? What I mean is, how important will they be to us?' The questioner was a stocky, deeply sunburned man who wore the uniform and insignia of a full colonel in the United States Army. He was General Groves' chief of staff, who had arrived in Paris the day before to help co-ordinate the final drive to round up as many enemy scientists as possible.

Sampson consulted his folder. 'The names don't mean a great deal to me,' he replied, 'but then, I am not a scientist. They are Professors Walter Gorbach, Hans Strasser and Friedrich Weiz.'

One of the civilians at the table, who had been quietly smoking his pipe, nodded and spoke for the first time.

'I know of them all. Gorbach is the leading specialist in the separation of uranium isotopes, and published a paper on the subject just before the war which has been of considerable value in our own researches. The other two have both devoted years to investigating the potential explosive properties of Element 94, which we Americans now call plutonium. Yes, they are important, make no mistake about that.'

The sunburned American colonel looked hard at the man who had just spoken.

'Suppose the Russians were to begin an atomic research project now,' he said. 'How long would it take them to reach our own level? And how long would it take them with the assistance of enemy scientists of the calibre of these three?'

The other sucked at the stem of his pipe and thought carefully for a few moments before answering.

'Assuming that they were starting from scratch, and taking into account what we know of their scientific resources at the present time, it would probably take them about fifteen years from now.'

'Yes, yes,' the colonel said brusquely. 'And with top German help?'

The man on the other side of the table looked even more pensive, and paused again before offering his opinion.

'With their help, then — the Russians would probably have an atomic bomb by 1950.'

The colonel slapped both hands, palm down, on the table top. 'So there we have it. Three men who have the power to advance the Soviets' atomic research programme by something like ten years are on the loose, and we haven't the faintest idea of their whereabouts except that they are probably in Berlin, that is if they aren't dead. The question is, what can we do to lay our hands on them?'

Air Commodore Sampson cleared his throat, as though to express irritation at the American's forthright approach.

'There isn't a great deal we can do at the moment, colonel,' he commented mildly. 'As things stand, it looks very much as though the Russians will be in Berlin within the next few days, and we can't very well ask for their help, can we?'

Freddie Barnes looked with admiration at Sampson, aware that the air commodore was very much in command of the situation.

'Everything hinges,' Sampson continued, 'on the time it takes for Anglo-American forces to reach Berlin, and it may be longer than we think. There is little doubt that the Russians will occupy the city, and there is a strong possibility that, for political reasons, the British and Americans will be ordered to halt for the time being on the line of the River Elbe. Just how soon we shall be able to send a military mission into the enemy capital is anyone's guess, but you may be sure that when we do, Alsos specialists will be part of it. The problem then will be where to start looking.'

The air commodore shuffled his papers together and closed the folder.

'In the meantime,' he concluded, 'we can only hope that our SOE agent is still to some extent in command of the situation, and is in a position to forestall any move to hand over the scientists to the Russians until our representatives reach the capital. It's a long shot, but it's the most we can anticipate.'

Another man seated at the table, a commander in the Royal Navy, spoke for the first time.

'But there's no guarantee that they are in Berlin,' he objected. 'It's all conjecture. They could be anywhere. It's my guess that they've been recaptured and shot.'

'In which case,' Sampson said gravely, 'we do not have a problem. We must, however, continue to assume that they are still alive, until we hear anything to the contrary, and take action accordingly.'

With an abrupt gesture, the air commodore pushed the folder into the briefcase and stood up.

'Now, gentlemen, if there are no questions ... ? Good. We all have a great deal to do. I wish you all good luck. Let us hope that matters now move to a speedy conclusion, and that when we next meet it will be face to face with the enemy scientists — all of them.'

The conference broke up, those present going their separate ways. Barnes, anxious to get back to Rheine as soon as possible, caught a USAAF C-47 as far as Brussels and then hopped on to a 'mail run' RAF Anson to his destination early the following morning and was at work in his office by nine o'clock, catching up on the latest Intelligence reports. Most of the others who had been at the conference headed for Stadtilm, to see for themselves what Colonel Pash's team had discovered and to analyse the captured information in their own specialist fashions.

The exception was Air Commodore Sampson, who took a communications flight directly back to London, where he was to report of the Director of Scientific Intelligence at the Air Ministry.

For Sampson, it was a thoughtful journey. He was preoccupied not so much with the missing enemy scientists, but with thoughts of the Special Operations Executive agent who had escaped with them and whose identity was known only to a handful of select people. The agent was a very special operative who, until presumed killed in the Mosquito attack on the Abwehr headquarters, had been into occupied Europe several times since 1942 — but not many people were aware of that.

Not even her fiancé, Wing Commander George Yeoman.

Chapter Six

FOR NO. 505 SQUADRON, THE THIRD WEEK OF APRIL GOT AWAY to a bad start. It began when, on the very first sortie flown on Sunday the twenty-second, Phil Trussler's Meteor failed to develop full power on take-off and ran off the end of the runway, plunging into a swamp and breaking up.

The accident happened almost under the nose of the startled runway controller, who leaped from his caravan and sprinted over to the scene of the crash. There was little that could be done; the Meteor's wings, tail unit and bits of fuselage were lying on the surface of the morass, but of the nose section and cockpit there was no sign.

'Well, that's that,' the runway controller muttered to the crew of a fire tender that came racing up to the spot. 'They'll never find the body.'

At that moment, with a gurgling, sucking noise, a hideous apparition came grovelling up out of the mud. Completely covered in black slime, it flopped its way across the swamp, half swimming, half crawling, until it reached a patch of relatively dry ground, where it lay gasping and snorting like a stranded seal. A few moments later it sat upright and reached up with mud-encrusted hands to pull aside a flying helmet, revealing the outraged and slightly bruised features of the pilot.

'You bastards,' he croaked, 'don't just stand there! Get a bloody rope, or something, and get me out of here!'

By the time a rope had been produced and thrown to Trussler, who was then dragged unceremoniously to the edge of the swamp, Yeoman had arrived, fearing the worst. At the sight of Trussler's plight, and on learning that the young pilot was uninjured apart from a few bruises, the wing commander doubled over in helpless laughter, wrinkling his nose.

'God, Phil, you stink to high heaven! We really thought you'd had it, when we saw you go in like that.'

'I was lucky,' Trussler grunted. 'I suppose I must have been knocked out for a second or two, because when I woke up everything was dark — I was completely buried in muck. I had the sense to undo my straps, then I just struck out instinctively. There wasn't really much cockpit left — it must have broken up in the crash — to I started flailing my arms and legs like mad and somehow I got to the surface. My oxygen mask was still in place, so that prevented the mud getting into my nose and mouth, otherwise I would probably have choked.'

Trussler was none the worse for his experience in the evil-smelling mud, although for several days afterwards people ostentatiously held their noses whenever he came near them. In the way of accidents, however, much worse was to follow.

The next day, a pair of Meteors flown by Pilot Officer Bedell and Sergeant Hartley took off to carry out a defensive patrol in the Oldenburg sector, where Second Army units were pushing towards Bremerhaven and Wilhelmshaven. They never returned, and it was long after dark before word of their fate reached Rheine via HQ 83 Group.

About an hour before sunset, the two Meteors had been sighted near Cloppenburg, presumably on their way home, by British ground forces. The two jets had been seen to enter cloud in close formation, and a few moments later the troops had heard a big explosion and seen debris fluttering down. It had been impossible to carry out a search, because the wreckage had fallen into a wood and darkness had intervened.

Yeoman drove out to the scene the following morning with Wing Commander Burns, the senior technical officer at Rheine, and a small team of investigators, to be shown the crash site by army officers. The wreckage of the two jets was scattered over a wide area, and the undergrowth in which it had fallen still smouldered gently.

Part of one pilot had been recovered, and soldiers were still looking for the rest of him. The remains found so far were lying on a purple sheet, looking like chunks of half cooked meat; it was impossible to tell which man it was. The other pilot, presumably, was lying pulped under a ball of scorched metal that had been the nose section of his Meteor; it had gouged a deep crater among the trees, and troops were digging their way into it.

There was no doubt at all that the two dead pilots had been the victims of a mid-air collision, but what had caused it was a different matter. It was now up to the experts to work out whether the aircraft had collided in cloud as a result of pilot error, or whether mechanical failure in one of them — an explosion in a turbine, for example — had caused it to sheer brutally into the path of the other. Whatever the reason, it had been a singularly pointless way to die, especially now that the end of hostilities was in sight, and Yeoman felt sick at heart as he drove back to base. In a way, the accident seemed to negate the Squadron's earlier success, when its pilots had destroyed the enemy seaplanes.

Still feeling at a very low ebb, he ate a little lunch, attended to some paperwork and then wandered down to the Squadron's dispersal. No operations were scheduled for that afternoon, but one never knew.

He had a word with the pilots who were on standby and then went outside, sitting down on a grassy mound with his back to the dispersal hut. It was pleasantly warm for April and he felt himself beginning to relax in the sunshine as he took out his pipe and began to fill the bowl methodically.

He was still occupied by this task when a sudden movement caused him to look up sharply. For a moment he wondered what had caught his attention, then he saw what it was and smiled.

A few yards away, from its vantage point on top of a pile of stones, a tabby kitten regarded him quizzically, its head on one side. It was probably about six months old, he guessed, and to judge by its appearance either the hunting on Rheine airfield was not very good or else the cat was not yet experienced enough, for even at this distance he could see its ribs showing beneath its fur.

Yeoman called softly to it and it flattened itself full length on the stones, its tail flicking from side to side. He called again and the cat disappeared, although he had an idea that it had not gone very far.

He got up and went into the dispersal hut. On a small table in one corner was the remains of someone's hasty meal; a half-eaten corned beef sandwich and a couple of biscuits. Yeoman crumbled the lot on to a tin plate, poured half a can of condensed milk over it, and set it down outside close to the pile of stones before resuming his vigil.

It was not long before the kitten poked its head over the stones again, its head turning this way and that. Yeoman could almost see its nose twitching as it scented the food, and he wondered how long it would take before the animal's hunger overcame its natural caution.

It was several minutes before the kitten decided that there was no immediate danger and began to venture cautiously down the pile of stones, stopping frequently to look around. Yeoman felt an almost childish sense of delight when it finally crept up to the edge of the plate and began to gorge itself, oblivious to everything now but the nourishment it was taking into its starved body.

'Oh, there you are, George. I've been looking for you.'

Yeoman looked up, startled, as Tim Phelan's shadow fell across him, and placed a finger over his lips.

'Don't frighten the poor little sod away, Tim,' he said, pointing to the gulping kitten. 'It's about on its last legs.'

Phelan grinned and bent forward, hands on knees, to look closely at the little cat.

'It obviously must have belonged to the Luftwaffe,' he said. 'Look — it's got a "H" marking on its head. That couldn't possibly stand for anything other than Hermann.'

And Hermann the cat was named, from then on. It became Yeoman's personal pet, allowing no one else to touch it, and the unofficial mascot of 505 Squadron. In the days to come, it grew exceedingly fat.

In a strange way, the sudden arrival of the kitten into Yeoman's life did much to lift his depression. He stood up, dusting down his uniform, and faced his second-in-command.

'You said you'd been looking for me, Tim. Any particular reason?'

'Just that Group Captain Kingston wants to see you. Something about laying on a Meteor demonstration flight for some American Air Force blokes — I think it's at one of their airfields in France.' The Irishman looked at Yeoman hopefully. 'If you want someone to do it, I'm volunteering,' he said. 'I have erotic dreams about steak and ice-cream.'

Phelan, however, was destined to be disappointed, for Group HQ had specifically asked for the demonstration to be carried out by Yeoman himself. Early the following morning, therefore, he took off and set course south-westwards, heading for Brussels; jet fuel was available there and he planned to top up his tanks before flying on to his destination, the airfield of Cambrai-Epinoy. After the demonstration, he would have plenty of fuel left to get back to Brussels and fill his tanks again before the return flight to Rheine.

Jet fighters were no longer a source of interest to the personnel at Brussels-Evère, for by now RAF Meteors en route to the three front-line jet squadrons had become a familiar sight as they dropped in to refuel. Within half an hour of landing there Yeoman was once more on his way, circling once over the ancient spires of the Belgian capital before turning the Meteor's nose southwards on the last short leg of his journey into France.

Yeoman took the fighter in a fast climb up to fifteen thousand feet and settled down to enjoy the ten-minute flight, looking down through patches of drifting cloud at the chequered landscape. The cockpit of the aircraft in which he now sat, he reflected, was a far cry from that of the piston-engined Hawker Hurricane in which he had gone to war in these very skies nearly five years earlier, all but a few days. He had been a month over his twentieth birthday then, and he realized with a sudden shock that the years which had intervened represented only a small slice of his life: much less for example, than those he had spent at the venerable old grammar school, set among its woods by the riverside in Yorkshire's picturesque Swale-dale. Yet into those five years he had packed a lifetime; if he achieved nothing more in the years to come, his life would still have been well spent.

He had no regrets — except one, and he refused to let his mind dwell on that. Julia had been part of his life, and the war had taken her from him; but perhaps that was in a sense just, for it was the war that had brought them together in the first place. With sadness, he realized, not for the first time, how little he had really known about her; in the times they had been together she had spoken only briefly about her work as a war correspondent for the *New York Globe*, and had never referred at all to the assignments that had taken her away for lengthy periods. About her family and friends in America, he knew next to nothing. He did not even know where, or how, she had met her death.

Damn it, he told himself, forget it. What the hell was Cambrai's call-sign? He found it, written on the back of his hand, and turned his radio to the appropriate frequency.

'Big Ball, this is Blow Job 14. How do you hear me?'

'Loud and clear, Blow Job 14.' The voice was slow, American and very precise. Yeoman smiled to himself and pressed the R/T transmit button again.

'Blow Job 14 is five miles north-east of the field, descending from angels one-five. Would you like me to make a low run?'

After a short pause, the American voice replied: 'Okay, 14, that's approved. Make your run from east to west along Runway two-eight.

The QFE is one-zero-one-five millibars and the surface wind two-four-zero degrees at ten knots.'

Yeoman acknowledged, looking ahead. Cambrai-Epinoy was clearly visible through his windscreen, and he could see that the airfield was packed with aircraft, their uncamouflaged metal surfaces glittering in the sunshine. After being used to the drab grey-green camouflage of the RAF'S machines, such a sight seemed peculiar in wartime; but at the heights the Americans operated camouflage was unimportant, and a highly-polished surface of natural metal could add a few vital knots to an aircraft's speed in combat.

He brought the Meteor round in a gentle curve, lining up with the main runway and losing height all the time. The whisper of the airflow over the nose grew louder as the speed built up to 400 knots; Yeoman was careful not to exceed this figure, for the Meteor was carrying its 180-gallon ventral fuel tank, which was only half empty, and was a corresponding limitation on the maximum diving speed.

Nevertheless, the Meteor's run across the airfield at less than fifty feet was impressive enough, the jet fighter hurling up the main runway like a bullet, trailing the screech of its engines behind it, before pulling into an upward roll that took it vertically through a layer of drifting cloud. Lost to sight momentarily, it reappeared in a descending turn towards the end of the runway, with flaps fully extended and undercarriage down. A couple of minutes later Yeoman touched down neatly and taxied clear of the runway, following a jeep that led him towards the dispersal area.

An airman wearing yellow overalls and a blue baseball cap marshalled the Meteor to its parking place at the end of a line of P-51 Mustang fighters. Yeoman shut down the engines, carried out his post-flight checks and climbed down from the cockpit, walking round the end of the wing to meet a small group of senior officers who had been awaiting his arrival on the tarmac.

The first of them, a lean man who wore the insignia of a full colonel and who stood almost a head taller than Yeoman, approached with hand outstretched, a broad smile on his face. On the left breast of his uniform he wore three rows of medal ribbons, including the British Distinguished Flying Cross, surmounted by the USAAF flying badge, while the right breast sported the pilot's wings of the RAF. He seized Yeoman's hand and pumped it vigorously.

'Good to see you, George. I see you've lost none of the old flair.'

Yeoman looked at the tall American with great affection. His friendship with Jim Callender was almost as old as his association with the RAF, for Callender — long before America's entry into the war — had crossed the Atlantic to fly and fight for the British, and the two men had served together as sergeant pilots during the Battle of France in 1940. Callender had later commanded one of the 'Eagle Squadrons' — RAF units composed of American volunteers — before being transferred to the USAAF at the end of 1942. The transfer had been very much against his will, but at that time the United States 8th Army Air Force had been only just beginning to build up its resources in Britain, and men with Jim Callender's kind of combat experience had been desperately needed.

Yeoman knew that Callender had recently been appointed base commander at Cambrai, and for that reason alone he had welcomed the opportunity to make this visit. Their meetings had been all too infrequent over the past few years.

Callender introduced Yeoman to the men who accompanied him. They included a couple of one-star generals, a us Senator who was on a 'fact-finding tour' of the USAAF bases in France, the commanders of the P-51 squadrons at Cambrai and a harrassed-looking RAF group captain who was apparently some sort of liaison officer at the Joint Allied Air HQ in Paris. He kept looking at his watch and muttering that he wished the bar was open.

The Americans — especially the P-51 pilots — showed a keen interest in the Meteor, and Yeoman spent the next half hour showing them round the aircraft, answering their spate of questions as well as he was able. Callender was impressed by the compact simplicity of the jet fighter's cockpit and told Yeoman that he, too, had had an opportunity to fly a jet aircraft when he was last in the United States a few months earlier.

'The Lockheed P-80, they call it,' he explained. 'I went across to Burbank — that's the Lockheed test field in California — and flew one twice in January. She's a really sweet little ship, George. The guys over there call her the Shooting Star. As a matter of fact, Lockheeds are angling for me to join their team after the war, and I've got to admit I'm thinking about it seriously. They've got some first-rate guys, including

Dick Bong — he's the fellow who shot down forty Japs in the Pacific — and some pretty interesting projects on the drawing board.'

Later, over lunch, Callender told Yeoman that he had also flown several captured German aircraft — much to the RAF pilot's envy, for so far such an opportunity had not come his way.

'Damn near killed myself in a Messerschmitt 109,' the American grunted. 'I tried to fly it like I would a P-51 — you know, a nice tight circuit, with a steady turn all the way down until you're over the end of the runway, levelling out just before touchdown. Christ, man, I was in a turn that wasn't anywhere near tight, descending left-handed with about 150 knots on the clock, when the bloody thing went berserk and tried to turn itself upside down. God knows how I managed to recover before I hit the deck; I'll swear my port wingtip touched the grass. Anyway, I rammed on full throttle and climbed to about ten thousand feet, where I flew around in circles for a while, quietly crapping myself. Then I realized what I'd done — in my excitement at flying a Hun kite, I'd completely forgotten that the airspeed was calibrated in kilometres per hour. I had, in fact, been turning at about ninety knots instead of 150; small wonder that the damn thing tried to flick itself into the ground.'

Yeoman smiled. Knowing Callender of old, he could never tell how much of the irrepressible American's tales were what the RAF classed as a 'line shoot'.

Suddenly, Callender became serious. 'George,' he asked, 'have you come across any Me 262s?'

'Not personally,' Yeoman replied. 'Some of the chaps encountered them when the Squadron was flying Tempests a few months ago and even managed to shoot a couple down, but they were the devil's own job to catch and we didn't have much hope of attacking them on their own airfields either, because of the flak. We haven't seen any since we've been flying Meteors. Why do you ask?'

Callender chewed on a piece of steak before replying. 'Just curiosity, that's all. We've had a lot of trouble with the bastards. We were escorting a B-17 mission to Magdeburg a few days ago and they really ripped into us. I wasn't on the show myself, but the guys said that the 262s were firing rockets. One of our groups lost four P-51s, not to mention the bomber losses. We just can't catch the goddamn things. You've got to admit, George, that they're streets ahead of us.'

Yeoman nodded. 'Yes, the 2nd Tactical Air Force fighter-bomber boys had a real problem with them, too, when the 262s first appeared in any numbers last autumn. The jets would cruise around at low level until they sighted a formation of our chaps, then they'd make a fast climbing attack from beneath. I remember talking to the co of one of our Spitfire squadrons, whose boys were bounced by a solitary 262 over Holland; he came straight up from under them, shot one of them down, and then — to add insult to injury — the bastard carried out a series of upward rolls as he climbed away into the clouds. There wasn't a damn' thing anyone could do about it.'

The two generals and the senator had been listening with rapt interest to this conversation, and the senator had been making furious notes on the back of a menu. Now he coughed loudly, interrupting their exchange, and leaned across the table to address Yeoman.

'Say there, er' — he wrestled with Yeoman's unfamiliar rank for a moment, then got it right — 'say, Wing Commander, what about the guys who fly those enemy jets? I guess they aren't anything like as good as our people?'

Yeoman and Callender looked wordlessly at one another, then the RAF pilot said quietly:

'As a matter of fact they're every bit as good, and in many cases better.'

The senator looked offended, so Yeoman went on to explain that he was not referring to the rank and file — the scrapings of the manpower barrel which Germany had been forced to throw into the fight over the past few months.

'I'm talking about the professionals — the fighter leaders who have been in action almost continuously since the very beginning. And by that I mean since the invasion of Poland in 1939, more than two years before America entered the war. I don't mean anything derogatory by that statement; I'm just trying to prove that these men are highly experienced, and therefore dangerous. That's why they have survived. Make no mistake about it; they know everything there is to know about air combat — and don't forget that for months now they have been operating under incredibly adverse conditions, which makes their continued success story all the more remarkable. Let me show you a typical example.'

He reached into the pocket of his tunic and pulled out a wallet, from which he extracted a folded piece of paper. Smoothing it out, he handed it to the senator, who long-sightedly studied it at arms length.

'What you are looking at, sir,' Yeoman explained, 'is a photograph of one of the men I've just been talking about. His name is Colonel Joachim Richter, and it seems probable that our paths may have crossed on more than one occasion. The article that went with the photo, which appeared in a Swiss aviation magazine, said that Richter had fought in France, Russia, the Balkans and the Mediterranean. His decorations are impressive, and so is his score — over one hundred enemy aircraft destroyed at the time of writing, which was last year.'

'A hundred?' the senator interrupted. 'Surely that's rather excessive?' There was a slightly derisory smile on his lips which Yeoman found most irritating.

'Not at all,' he said calmly. 'Most of their top men have over a hundred kills to their credit, although admittedly most of them seem to have been scored on the Russian Front. He retrieved the photograph and put it away carefully.

'Anyway,' he continued, 'our Intelligence people have done a pretty thorough job on Richter, who in fact was the last Luftwaffe commander at Rheine, where my squadron is now based. There are indications that he is now commanding a Wing of Me 262s, and that his pilots are veterans of pretty much the same calibre.'

He patted his tunic pocket. 'I keep this picture for one reason: to remind myself of the kind of men who are still flying and fighting for the Luftwaffe. It's a kind of insurance against becoming complacent, even at this late stage.'

The senator snorted. 'I must say, Wing Commander, that I'm amazed by your — your comradely attitude towards this fellow. He is, after all, your enemy and an enemy of freedom. A Nazi, too.'

'No one has ever said that he's a Nazi,' Yeoman pointed out. 'All I'm saying is that he is a professional, and one hell of a good pilot; he has to be, or he wouldn't still be around. I hope he survives the war; I'd like very much to meet him.'

The senator opened his mouth to make a retort and Callender, realizing that Yeoman was starting to get angry, hurriedly changed the subject. Afterwards, Callender took the Englishman to one side.

'Sorry about that George. I should have made sure that fat bastard was sitting at the other end of the table. These politicians are an infernal nuisance. They believe every damn thing they read in the papers, and then make the rest of us out to be little more than liars. I remember once, a couple of years ago, a senator came out to England when I was commanding a Thunderbolt group and demanded to know why our boys were still being shot down. I asked him what the hell he was talking about, and he said that the Germans didn't have any fighters left. They couldn't have, because the papers said that we'd destroyed two thousand of them in one week, and the papers had to be right. And that was in the middle of 1943, when the Huns were beating seven kinds of shit out of our daylight bomber formations!'

The two men went into the anteroom of Epinoy's spacious mess and spent a pleasant hour reminiscing over a pot of coffee. The American generals, the senator and the RAF group captain mercifully left them alone, having disappeared into the bar, but after a while they were joined by one or two of the P-51 squadron commanders, who with typical American forthrightness began to question Yeoman about his flying career and to bombard him with technical questions about the types of aircraft he had flown. It was something of a relief when, at 1430, the time came for him to carry out his flying display.

Callender gave Yeoman a lift down to the flight line, where the RAF pilot made the customary external checks of his aircraft before preparing to climb up into the cockpit. He noticed that a row of deckchairs had been placed in front of the control tower, sheltered from the slight breeze, and that the senator and his entourage were reclining comfortably in them — so comfortably in fact, that the senator appeared to be asleep.

'Probably pissed,' Callender grinned. 'Never mind, George, I'm sure you'll do your damndest to wake him up. Have a good trip back. See you when the war's over.'

Yeoman would never know what effect, if any, the ear-shattering low run over the airfield with which he began his display had on the senator. For ten minutes he looped, rolled and dived the jet fighter across Epinoy, streaking along the main runway at high speed and then cruising past the audience as slowly as the Meteor would safely go, with wheels and flaps extended, before completing the show with a meticulous four-point hesitation roll and climbing away into the north-eastern sky towards Evère.

A couple of hours later, after refuelling in Belgium, he touched down at Rheine to find everything in a state of feverish agitation. In his absence, orders had come through for the squadron to move up to a new location at Celle. It was to be a temporary detachment, but it was one the pilots greeted with tremendous enthusiasm. From Celle, the Meteors could, if so ordered, easily extend their offensive patrols to cover the last great German bastion of all: Berlin itself.

Chapter Seven

BERLIN WAS DYING.

Eight Soviet armies, four of them tank armies, were closing in on the city. On 24 April, the Russians threw everything they had to complete the ring of fire and steel around the capital; in the north and east their spearheads had already reached the last defensive ring before the city centre, while in the south-east shock troops of the 1st Belorussian and 1st Ukrainian Fronts met at Bohnsdorf, isolating and encircling the remnants of the German 9th Army. Meanwhile, the 4th Guards Tank Army had reached the lakes that flanked Potsdam and the 2nd Guards Tank Army, spearing down from the north, was threatening Spandau.

On that same day, American and Russian forces were rushing to join together at Torgau on the River Elbe, effectively cutting what was left of Nazi Germany in two.

The Thousand-Year Reich was sliding to devastating, flaming ruin, nine hundred and eighty-eight years too soon. The battle was lost. It would already have been abandoned had it not been for the wild hopes of one man, who, half paralysed, prematurely old and buried in tomb-like silence in a bunker twenty feet under the debris of Berlin, still commanded the obedience of his dwindling band of henchmen.

Only in the west, where the bridges spanned the river Havel at Spandau, was an escape route still open out of the shattered city. Civilian refugees still poured across them, desperate to get away before the steel jaws of the Russian trap clamped down on them. In Berlin itself, what was left of the 56th Panzer Corps, supported by fanatical SS and Hitler Youth formations — and a few battalions of tired and dispirited old men who made up the Volkssturm, or Home Guard — prepared to sacrifice their lives in a hopeless last-ditch defence of the city centre. Berlin was no Stalingrad; fanaticism and terror might prolong the dying agonies for a few days, but no more.

Above the rubble of Berlin rose four huge flak towers, their hundred-foot columns standing like monuments amid the drifting smoke. Since the twentieth — Hitler's birthday — the crews of these towers had had a grandstand view, unobstructed now by any tall buildings, of Russian artillery moving into position for the final assault some miles away. The towers were equipped with twin 128-mm guns, mounted on concrete platforms, and for four days they had been carrying out an artillery duel with the Russians. Now on the twenty-fourth, the great guns were silent, for the crews were husbanding their dwindling stocks of ammunition to play their part in the final defence. Communications had long since broken down and the crews no longer had any idea where to direct their fire.

Ritcher had just visited one of the flak towers to see for himself how the situation around Berlin was developing, and was making his way back towards the Reichs Chancellery across the wreckage of the Tiergarten during an unexpected lull in the Russian shelling when he came upon the soldiers. There were about thirty of them, commanded by a major who did not appear to have shaved for days and who was swaying on his feet with fatigue. He accosted Richter and saluted wearily, identifying himself and his unit.

The major explained that he and his men had been on the north-west sector when they had suddenly been ordered across Berlin to help in the defence of Tempelhof airport. Two days earlier, he told Richter bitterly, he had commanded a hundred men; these were the sorry remnant.

Richter looked at the soldiers. Most of them seemed to be no more than fifteen or sixteen years old. Many were white-faced and trembling with fear. One other officer was present; a young lieutenant of about eighteen.

The major asked Richter if he had seen any other men from the same unit pass this way, and Richter replied that he had not. He also pointed out that most of the roads between the Tiergarten and Tempelhof were hopelessly blocked by rubble.

Suddenly, the young lieutenant began to cry. There was no sound, but his shoulders trembled and Richter could see tears coursing down the boy's cheeks, although he tilted his steel helmet over his eyes and made a valiant effort to hide his emotions. The men looked at him dully, then looked away. Many of them looked ready to burst into tears themselves.

'Shut up, Gustav,' the major said, although there was only weary resignation in his tone. Turning back to Richter, he went on:

'We're done for. There'll be no relief. All this talk about linking up with General Wenck's Berlin Relief Column — it's a load of crap. They've been telling us that story about Wenck for weeks now. Who the hell do they think we are? Wenck won't come. God alone knows where he is. The Russians are swarming everywhere; they're just playing cat and mouse with us. And we are told to go on fighting to the last man — or rather the last little boy,' he corrected himself, glancing almost contemptuously at the remains of his command and the weeping lieutenant.

The major gave a sudden sigh of resignation and straightened his drooping shoulders, adjusting the position of his webbing and cradling his machine-pistol in the crook of his arm like a farmer out for a Saturday afternoon shoot. He faced his men and rapped out a curt command, bringing them into a semblance of military order. As they marched off across the Tiergarten, past the emergency landing strip with its carcases of wrecked communications aircraft, the major waved briefly to Richter.

'So long, Colonel. See you in Siberia.'

Richter picked his way through the rubble and returned quickly to the Chancellery, where General Roller had set up a temporary Air HQ in one of the underground offices adjoining Hitler's bunker. The main Luftwaffe HQ at Wildpark-Werder, on the other side of the Havel, had been evacuated twenty-four hours earlier under the threat of the rapidly approaching Soviet spearheads; the latter had already overrun the army communications centre at Zossen, effectively severing Berlin's landline links with the outside world. Communications were now maintained, after a fashion, by VHF line-of-sight radio equipment, the signals transmitted from a captive balloon.

General Roller was no longer in Berlin; on the twenty-third he had flown out of the besieged capital to report to Hermann Göring at Command Post B, the secondary military headquarters near Munich, leaving General Eckhardt Christian as the Luftwaffe liaison officer at Führer Headquarters.

Christian, and Richter too, were both aware of the real reason behind Roller's flight south. On 22 April a Panzer Corps under the ss General Steiner, was to have launched a major counter-attack north of Berlin.

Steiner knew that such an attack was impossible, and said so; Hitler's retort was furious and to the point.

'Officers who do not accept this order without reservation are to be arrested and shot instantly. You yourself I make responsible with your head for its execution ... any commander who has orders to send troops to you and who holds them back will be a dead man within five hours.'

But by the late afternoon of the twenty-second Steiner still had not counter-attacked, and during his daily situation conference Hitler broke down completely. Convinced now that Steiner would never attack he collapsed in a tearful, storming rage, as though realizing for the first time the awful inevitability of Berlin's fate.

Most of his acolytes were there. Feldmarschall Keitel, with his dead fish's eyes, contemptuously dubbed 'Lakaitel' (Little Lackey) by his subordinates; Jodl, also a yes-man; Burgdorf, Krebs, now commanding phantom armies; the treacherous Martin Bormann, Nazi Party Secretary- and many others, like participants at some hellish black sabbath. Now even they stared, aghast, as the Führer's mouth fell open and the pale eyes stared crazily at them.

'I have been deceived by the SS ... I never expected this from my SS!' The whimper was pathetic, nauseating to those who heard it and who had been with this shadow of a man through the times when the power of his oratory commanded millions.

The whimper died away and Hitler sprang to his feet, clutching the back of his chair, screaming maniacally at those who had served him.

'Deceivers, scoundrels, villains, serpents! I have nurtured deceitful serpents in my bosom! Nothing but treachery and failure as far as one can see ... Corruption on every hand ... lies, lies, lies! Every general is a traitor and deserves to die ... the Luftwaffe is no better ... all soldiers are cowards, the German people inadequate ... '

And so it went on, for minutes that seemed like hours, before the Führer exhausted himself. At last, quite calmly, he announced that he would remain in Berlin to the end and kill himself before the Russians could take him prisoner. He ordered all his papers and records to be taken out and burned.

Bormann, Keitel and Jodl all tried to persuade Hitler to leave Berlin on the grounds that it was impossible to exercise command from there any more. He refused, and so Keitel and Jodl pledged themselves to remain with him. So did his propaganda minister, Josef Goebbels, dog-faithful to the end with his wife and six children.

Only General Koller flew out to Munich, but not for reasons of personal safety. His self-imposed task was to report on Hitler's breakdown to Hermann Göring, the Luftwaffe C-in-C, who had been designated Deputy Führer. Göring, would know what to do, for it was clear that Hitler was no longer rational.

On the night of the twenty-fourth, Russian bombers and artillery carpeted Berlin from end to end with a deluge of high explosive. In the underground bunker, Richter, von Gleiwitz and the other officers of Koller's staff — or rather Christian's staff, in Koller's absence — knew that they were completely safe from the bombs and shells, although it was unnerving enough to feel, rather than hear, the concussions that were transmitted through the earth. At least they were more fortunate than the poor devils outside; the Berliners who had not fled had become a city of troglodytes, half out of their minds with fear for the present — and for the immediate future, for refugees from east Prussia had brought with them horrifying stories of Russia rape and atrocity.

Yet even now, the Berliners had not lost their cynical sense of humour.

'Better a Russian on the belly than a bomb on the head,' was the grim joke that passed among the endless food queues, which formed magically in the brief intervals between the shelling.

Shortly after dawn the next day, Richter and von Gleiwitz ventured out of the bunker to stretch their aching limbs, cramped by long hours of inactivity in the relatively small shelter.

The scene that met their eyes was from the darkest depths of a hideous nightmare, but from this nightmare there was no awakening. All around, buildings were in flames; the air was thick with acrid smoke and clouds of gritty dust. Over everything there hung a cloying pall of death and decay, of corpses rotting beneath the rubble. The dead, victims of the previous day's bombardment, lay everywhere in obscene piles on the shattered pavements; the burial squads, if such existed any more, could no longer carry out their task.

Only the rats flourished. A huge grey specimen, its fur matted and obscene, crouched on a mound of rubble and stared at the two men, its button eyes glittering. Von Gleiwitz cursed and shied a stone at it, sending it scurrying away.

Richter glanced up as the roar of aero-engines sounded above the crackle of the flames and caught a brief glimpse of three aircraft sweeping low over the ruins, fleeting between the columns of smoke with anti-aircraft fire spitting ineffectually after them. They were Ilyushin Il-2 Sturmoviks, the ground-attack aircraft which the German Panzer crews on the eastern front had hated and feared more than anything else.

The sight caused a wave of longing to flood through Richter.

Never before had he felt so utterly helpless. That was where he belonged, in the sky, not here in this stinking concrete hell, trapped among madmen who spent their last days plotting counter-attacks by non-existent armies on their maps.

Von Gleiwitz was thinking the same thing; he could sense it. He looked directly at his adjutant and held his gaze.

'Hasso,' he said slowly and deliberately, so that there could be no misunderstanding, 'Hasso, we have to get out of here. Either south, to Munich, or west, towards the Elbe.'

Von Gleiwitz nodded slowly. 'I, too, have no desire to be captured by the Russians. But how are we to do it? Even if we manage to get clear of Berlin, the head-hunters are everywhere. They are executing anyone even remotely suspected of deserting his post.'

'We bide our time,' Richter said firmly. 'I am sure that an opportunity will present itself. The more confusion that exists, the better it will be for us.'

They returned to the bunker and set about their task of analysing the disjointed reports that filtered in from the units defending the Berlin perimeter. Some of the heaviest fighting was taking place in the south, in Sector D, which was held by the 'Müncheberg' Panzer Division. Its front lay across Tempelhof airfield, about four miles away from the city centre. The division had a dozen tanks and thirty armoured personnel carriers and was desperately short of manpower. Pleas for reinforcements resulted in a small influx of elderly Volkssturm men and any stragglers who could be rounded up.

By mid-morning, communications with the garrison at Tempelhof had broken down completely, and so Richter and von Gleiwitz volunteered to visit the front line in order to find out at first hand what was happening. Before they left the bunker, Richter insisted on being provided with written orders signed by General Christian; to move around Berlin without specific orders could mean a firing squad at the hands of roaming bands of ss 'police'.

motor-cycle combination and set off southwards down the Wilhelmstrasse, making frequent detours to avoid mountains of fallen masonry. Mentally, Richter blessed Berlin's architects; had the avenues they had designed been less broad, the rubble would have made them completely impassable. As it was they were able to make progress, although not without difficulty. Apart from natural obstacles, they were forced to stop from time to time to take cover from shellfire and the low-flying fighter-bombers that swooped down to strafe the ruins, apparently at random.

They turned on to the Blücherstrasse, at the far end of which an artillery battery was in position. Beyond it, past the Lilienthalstrasse and the cemetery intersected by it, was the airport.

The cemetery, in which German troops had set up defensive positions, had been fiercely shelled and bombed. The dead had been disinterred, their bones and splintered coffins scattered to the winds. Neat rows of trees had once flanked the roads that wound their way through the big graveyard, but these, like the beautiful old oaks and beeches in the adjacent Hasenheide Park, had been stripped and ravaged by blast and shrapnel.

To his surprise, the first officer Richter encountered as he entered the command post on the northern edge of the airport was the major with whom he had spoken in the Tiergarten the previous morning.

'I see you made it, then,' Richter said, shaking hands with the man. The major nodded.

'Yes, I made it. Gerhard didn't, though. You know — my lieutenant. Ha, ha.' The laugh was more than a little crazy. 'He tried to make a run for it. They caught him and strung him up from a girder in the Kreuzbergstrasse. They pinned a notice to his chest. Do you know what it said? It said: "Filthy cowards and defeatists, we've got them all on our lists." They made us watch while he died. The bastards! Gustav won the Iron Cross outside Lodz just after his seventeenth birthday.'

The major passed a weary hand over his eyes, then seemed to compose himself. In a low, even voice, he said:

'You want information on the position here, Colonel? Right, then, here it is. The Russian artillery shelled us without let-up all day yesterday, right up to dark. We asked for infantry reinforcements, and all we got were motley recruits like the kids I brought here myself yesterday morning. Most of them are dead now, incidentally. Behind the lines, everything is clogged by civilians, still trying to get away right under the Russian guns, dragging along some miserable bundle holding all they have left in the world. Haven't you see them, Colonel?'

Richter nodded. The major was telling him nothing that he did not already know, but he steeled himself to be patient. The man was clearly on the verge of collapse and was fingering his machine-pistol in a nervous manner. Anything might happen.

The major stared at him. 'Then how about this, Colonel? There are some houses on the far side of the airfield. The civilians were still in them — they must have chosen to stay and wait for the fighting to pass over them, rather than run away. Well, the Russians burned their way into those houses with flame-throwers last night. Through our binoculars we could see the people running from their homes. Women and kids. In flames. Screaming.'

'What is the material situation, Major?' Richter's interruption was deliberately harsh. He was hoping that the man's military training and inner discipline would react to the note of authority. It worked — for a few moments.

'Twelve tanks and thirty armoured cars, Colonel. I beg to report that these are the only armoured vehicles left in this sector. We were ordered to send the other tanks to other sectors, and they never returned. We have no vehicles left to transport our wounded to safety. I beg to inform the colonel that it is only the iron will of our commander, General Mummert, which has enabled the line to hold so far.'

Suddenly, the major's shoulders slumped again. 'Confusion,' he muttered. 'Order and counter-order. We have hardly any ammunition. This morning the division was ordered to move north to the Alexanderplatz, then the order was countermanded almost immediately, just before communications with the Chancellery ceased.'

He seized Richter's arm. 'Get out now, Colonel,' he hissed. 'You've done your share, I can see that from your decorations. Don't wait to see General Mummert; he's at the other end of the sector and God knows when he'll be back. Listen — it's been quiet now for over an hour. We had a big tank assault early this morning, but nothing since then. Ivan is up to something, and when he comes we can't hold him. We're finished here. Go on — go back to the Chancellery and tell them that!'

Richter nodded and shook hands with the major before leaving. It was an uncanny feeling — shaking hands with a man who had resigned himself to the fact that he was going to die.

They got away only just in time. Behind them, Tempelhof erupted in a hellish din of explosions as the Russians pounded the German positions with artillery, mortars and the hated 'Stalin Organs' — multiple rocket batteries that poured missiles out of the sky with a fiendish, rending screech. Fresh smoke clouds boiled up, and under them men ran around like ants and died as the T-34 tanks rolled forward, their heavy machine-guns raking the ground in front of them, supported by waves of screaming infantry.

Fierce fighting raged in the streets around Tempelhof. In the glare of burning houses, the roads were littered with dead and dying civilians. Household pets ran around in terrified circles, crying piteously, and were slaughtered too in the merciless fire. Women, driven out of their minds by terror of mass rape, fled from cellar to cellar.

Orders came to take up new positions on the western edge of Sector D. Troops moved rapidly through the rubble, only to be met by withering machine-gun fire. The positions were already in Russian hands. Slowly, relentlessly, harrassed all the time by swarms of Russian fighter-bombers that worked over the dying city from end to end, the defenders of Sector D — what was left of them — were pushed north-westwards, towards the centre of Berlin.

Richter and von Gleiwitz arrived back at the Chancellery early in the afternoon, choked with smoke and dust, their uniforms encrusted with grime. Richter at once sought out General Christian and asked him if he should report directly to the operations room in the Führerbunker to give a first-hand account of what he had seen to the chiefs of staff.

Christian shook his head and drew Richter to one side. The pilot knew immediately that something was seriously wrong.

'Forget it, Richter,' Christian advised quietly. 'Things have been happening in your absence.' He glanced around to make sure that no one else was listening, then went on:

'As you know, General Roller flew off to meet Reichsmarschall Göring the day before yesterday. Well, apparently he informed the Reichsmarschall of the Führer's ... lapse, shall we call it. The result was that this morning, the Führer received a signal from Göring asking whether the latter, as Hitler's deputy, should now assume leadership of the Reich, including complete freedom to negotiate with the Allies.'

Christian pursed his lips. 'The reaction, my dear Richter, was entirely predictable, in my opinion. Our commander-in-chief, Reichsmarschall Hermann Göring, has now been stripped of all public offices and his arrest ordered by the ss — although his life is to be spared "as a mark of the Führer's generosity". Unquote. Ritter von Greim has been promoted to field marshal and is to take Göring's place, with immediate effect.'

There was a lengthy silence, and then Richter said: 'I think I know what you are telling me, sir. I think you are saying that we Luftwaffe officers — particularly those in the vicinity of the Fuhrer — had better tread warily from now on.'

Christian nodded. 'That is precisely what I am saying. So you see, Richter, it would be a waste of time making your report to the High Command on the true situation in the south of the city. No one would believe you, and you would risk being hauled outside and shot as a defeatist.' He shrugged in resignation.

'Let them think what they like,' he muttered. 'It's all too late, anyway. I'm sorry you have had a wasted and dangerous journey.'

Yet in the heart of the fanatical man in the Führerbunker, whose world was only days away from collapsing in ultimate ruin, hope still burned that a miracle would intervene, and that his dark gods would not desert him in the final hour. And when dawn broke on 26 April — a clear, spring dawn in which, amazingly, birds once again sang over shattered Berlin — it seemed that the miracle might yet happen.

Early in the morning, news reached the Führerbunker that the 12th Army had opened a strong counter-attack northeastwards at the tip of the twin lakes near Potsdam, while the 9th Army was attacking westwards to meet it. After they had joined, both armies were to advance on Berlin from the south.

What was more — and this, perhaps more than anything else, brought temporary joy to Hitler's heart — the SS General Steiner was at last attacking towards Berlin from north-west of Oranienburg with the 25th Panzer Grenadier Division, the 2nd Naval Division and the 7th Panzer Division. From his headquarters at Neu Roofen, Feldmarschall Jodi — who had left the Berlin pocket soon after the conference of the twenty-second — announced jubilantly that all movements designed to relieve the capital had either begun or were about to begin.

For what remained of the Nazi hierarchy in Berlin, Thursday 26 April was a day of hope. Hitler, once more exuding confidence, contacted Jodi and ordered him to hold the Elbe line against Montgomery while at the same time releasing forces to fight in the Berlin area. The vital ports of Emden, Wilhelmshaven and Wesermunde were to be held at all costs.

The Führer was not yet aware that Bremen had just fallen to the British.

To those more in touch with reality than the men in the Führerbunker, it was already clear that the operation to relieve Berlin was not going to succeed, and that it had never had a chance of succeeding. Steiner had enjoyed a limited success, advancing and capturing a small bridgehead on the Havel west of Oranienburg, but he had only the 25th Panzer Grenadier Division at his disposal. Of the other units he was supposed to have relied upon for the attack, the 2nd Naval Division was strung out along the railroads between Oranienburg and Stettin, unable to move because the Russians were poised to make a breakthrough in this sector; while the 7th Panzer Division, which had been evacuated from Danzig only days earlier by sea, had no vehicles with which to move out of its assembly area to the west of Neubrandenburg.

General Heinrici, commanding Army Group Vistula, of which Steiner's force formed part, urgently requested permission to divert the divisions from their fruitless assault to support the 3rd Panzer Army, whose last reserves were crumbling north of Berlin before the assault of the Soviet 2nd Belorussian Front. Feldmarschall Jodi refused: such a move would be contrary to the Führer's directive.

The 12th Army, too, was confronted by an impossible task. Its mission was to advance north-east towards Berlin, while at the same time confronting Montgomery's forces on the Elbe. It was in no position to assist the 9th Army, which began its breakout attempt at dawn on the

26th. It did so with pitifully few supplies, because all the Luftwaffe support it had been promised had been diverted to supply the Berlin garrison.

Only Wenck's xx Corps, due west of Berlin, had any real chance of pushing through to the capital, and Wenck — an anti-Nazi — had already decided that if he succeeded, he would hold the bridgehead long enough only to allow the maximum number of troops and civilians to escape to the west before turning round and following them with the thirty-thousand men of his own command.

Only fragments of the true situation reached the staff in the Chancellery, for communications were sporadic and those that came through usually presented a completely false picture. Richter and von Gleiwitz were better informed than most, for they took turns at helping to man the communications centre-ostensibly because they had nothing better to do, but in reality because both men had decided that any chance to escape from the besieged city might depend on an accurate knowledge of the events unfolding around it.

That evening, to everyone's astonishment, a little Fieseler Storch light aircraft touched down on the short ribbon of concrete that led up to the Brandenburg Gate, next to the burnt-out Reichstag. The machine was shot almost to ribbons and one of its two occupants was wounded in the foot. He was Colonel-General Ritter von Greim, Göring's newly-appointed successor. The aircraft's other occupant was a petite, fair-haired woman whom Richter recognized immediately as Hanna Reitsch, the legendary test pilot.

Richter had never particularly liked Hanna Reitsch, but now, as the story of her nightmare flight into Berlin unfolded, he felt nothing but admiration for her. In the early hours of the 26th, she and von Greim had flown to the German Air Ministry's test airfield at Rechlin from Munich, where von Greim had his HQ, to undertake the 'special mission' into Berlin. At Rechlin, they learned that no German aircraft had managed to fly into the capital for over two days. Gatow airfield, on the western edge of the city, was known to be still in German hands, but it was surrounded by the Russians and under continual shellfire. No one knew whether enough of its runways remained to allow an aircraft to land.

The plan was to fly into Gatow, and from there to make the final 'hop' to the Chancellery in the city centre. If they were to break through the ring of Russian anti-aircraft guns and fighters speed was essential, so for the flight into Gatow it was decided to use the fastest aircraft available: a Focke-Wulfe 190 fighter, specially modified to carry a passenger. The aircraft was to be flown by a Luftwaffe sergeant, with von Greim occupying the second seat. Hanna Reitsch had presented something of a problem, since there was no room for three people in the narrow cockpit. In the end, she had wormed her way feet first into a tiny, tunnel-like space in the rear of the fuselage, where she lay in complete darkness surrounded by oxygen cylinders and other odds and ends.

It was the most terrifying flight of her life. She told Richter that the noise had been terrific; she was totally unable to move and the metal objects that surrounded her pressed painfully into her body. The flight to Gatow lasted thirty minutes, which seemed like an eternity. Once, she thought that her last moment had come when the aircraft went into a screaming power-dive; later, she learned that the pilot had been avoiding Russian fighters.

They landed at Gatow amid a storm of Russian gunfire. Every aircraft on the field had been knocked out except one, a Fieseler Storch observation machine. Hanna and von Greim took off in it at 1800 hours, heading for the Brandenburg Gate, where they hoped to find a space big enough to land. Since Hanna had no experience of flying under fire, von Greim insisted on piloting the little aircraft — but Hanna made sure that she could reach the controls over his shoulders.

It was just as well that she did so. As the little machine skimmed through the murderous fire over the Grunewald, there was a sudden deafening bang and a yellow flame streaked back from the engine. At the same instant von Greim shouted that he had been hit; an armour-piercing bullet had smashed through his right foot. A moment later he slumped to one side, unconscious.

Hanna at once reached over his inert body, grabbing the controls and fighting to keep the aircraft twisting and turning to avoid most of the Russian fire. Outside the cockpit the whole sky seemed to be in flames as shell after shell exploded, sending wicked splinters slicing through wings and fuselage. White-hot bullets shattered the perspex of the cockpit, but by a miracle none of them struck Hanna. With sick fear, she noticed streams of fuel pouring from bullet-torn wing tanks; all it needed was a single incendiary bullet and the aircraft would disintegrate in a ball of flame. But the sturdy little machine flew on, still answering the controls, over the shattered suburbs of Berlin.

Gradually, as she neared the city centre, the Russian fire died away. Now, however, the smoke from burning buildings mushroomed up in sulphurous yellow clouds, making it impossible to see ahead. The ruins flashed past, dangerously close, as she followed her compass blindly, heading for a landmark she knew well: the huge flak tower in the Tiergarten. The little aircraft lurched and jolted in the turbulence that rose from the fires below, and her task of controlling it was made more difficult by von Greim, who kept regaining consciousness for a few seconds at a time and convulsively seizing the stick. Each time Hanna had to fight him off, and they came perilously close to diving into the sea of rubble and fire.

At last, almost exhausted, she saw the flak tower looming up through the smoke, and beyond it the broad avenue that ran from west to east through the centre of Berlin. She turned east, following the bomb-cratered ribbon of concrete, until she sighted the Brandenburg Gate.

She touched down close by the famous landmark and helped von Greim — who by this time had regained his senses — out of the aircraft. She bound his shattered foot as best she could and they sat there among the piles of masonry for a long time, choking in the swirling smoke, before a German army truck appeared, threading its way through the debris.

They were driven to Hitler's bunker, where von Greim's foot was operated on immediately. Afterwards, with the general still on a stretcher, they were taken for an audience with Hitler. It was only then that von Greim learned that he had been appointed to succeed Göring, and that he had been ordered to Berlin to confer with Hitler on the 'future dispositions of the Luftwaffe'. With sick certainty, both he and Hanna Reitsch knew that they had risked their lives for nothing.

Hanna Reitsch's story threw Richter into a mood of deep despondency. In his mind, there had been a half-formed plan that it might somehow be possible to find a light aircraft on one of Berlin's landing strips and fly it out before the Russians closed in completely, but now there seemed to be no hope whatsoever of carrying out such a scheme. There were no longer any airworthy machines in the areas of Berlin still controlled by the Germans, and even von Greim had no idea whether it would be possible for someone to fly in from outside and evacuate him to Austria, where he was supposed to assemble the remnants of the Luftwaffe for a last stand.

It was not in Richter's character, however, to remain despondent for long. One last chance remained. Soon — God only knew how soon — the Russians would be in the city centre, and there were plans to fight a desperate last-ditch battle around the Chancellery.

'We will have two allies,' he confided quietly to von Gleiwitz, 'confusion and darkness. We must be prepared, at the last moment, to slip away from the bunker and go into hiding somewhere among the ruins. Then, when the final assault takes place, we shall try and get through the Russian front line and make our way towards the west. If we can get as far as the western outskirts of Berlin, we might just have a chance of reaching the American lines. According to the latest reports, the Amis are fifty miles away. It's not too far, with luck on our side. You and I both know the country; we can travel at night and hole up somewhere during the day.'

He gripped von Gleiwitz's shoulder. 'We must not give up hope, Hasso. Neither of us is going to die in this hell-hole.'

*

Three and a half miles west of the Chancellery, in the cellar of a ruined house in the suburb of Charlottenburg, four more people were also desperately trying to cling to a shred of hope. Three of them were men — one elderly, one middle-aged, the other relatively young — and the fourth was a woman. She was young, but the hardship and fear that had accompanied three years of working as an agent of the Allied Special Operations Executive in occupied Europe had left their mark. So had Belsen, although she had been one of the lucky ones. Nevertheless, she would have nightmares about that place for the rest of her life.

She looked at the three civilians, sleeping in exhaustion, twitching fitfully and murmuring. They, too, had their nightmares. They were her mission, and she had yet to complete it. How, she had no idea as yet. She would wait for the tide of battle to roll over them, and then think of something.

She caressed the Schmeisser sub-machine-gun that lay on her lap. It was her constant companion. If the worst came to the worst, she would use it on the three sleeping men and then on herself, rather than be captured by either Germans or Russians. Everyone, now, was her enemy.

Her gaze shifted to a mound of fallen masonry that occupied one half of the cellar. Beneath it lay two men. Both had belonged to Red Orchestra, the communist underground organization that Hitler had tried hard, but never quite succeeded, to suppress.

Her mind went involuntarily, once again, over the events of the past few weeks. There had been a mass escape from Belsen, organized — as she now knew — by Red Orchestra, and many had died so that she and the three scientists might live. At first, safe in hiding for the time being, she had felt nothing but gratitude, until she had learned from a chance remark what the true purpose of her liberators was; to hand the three scientists over to the Russians.

She herself was to have been an added bonus, with her intimate knowledge of SOE tactics and strategy. Any information extracted from her would have been extremely useful to the Soviet secret police.

She tried to shut her mind to the dead men under the pile of rubble. She had killed them; judging her moment carefully, waiting until they were off their guard, she had seized the Schmeisser that belonged to one of them and in a single fluid movement had cocked the weapon and shot them both down. SOE had taught her to kill people like that, and in many other ways. It was almost ridiculously easy, after the first time. The first time was the hardest of all. After that it was easy — provided you were careful not to look at their faces while you killed them.

Deliberately, she forced her thoughts away from the dark, stinking confines of the cellar and let them wing freely across the months and years, back to happier days. It helped to keep her sane, and God knew she had been close enough to losing her sanity on more than one occasion.

She wondered, for the thousandth time, if George Yeoman was still alive, and if so, whether he had been officially informed that she was dead. She thought it likely, for that was the way SOE operated, although she had no idea what excuse for her death they might have concocted. And she had no reason to suspect that SOE believed her to be anything other than dead.

The fact that she might still die no longer troubled her. For even if by some miracle she survived, and Yeoman survived, she doubted whether their relationship could be as it had been in those days, an age ago, when they had held each other and been full of hope.

Somewhere overhead, a Russian artillery barrage thundered, bringing dust trickling down from the cellar roof. In the cold darkness, Julia Connors turned her face to the rough stone and wept silently; but the tears were not for herself.

Chapter Eight

YEOMAN SAT WITH HIS BACK AGAINST A LARGE WOODEN packing-case which, according to the legend stencilled on its side, had once contained spare parts for Rolls-Royce Merlin engines. Hermann, the cat, lay half across his legs, with one eye open; the animal had adapted remarkably well to the move to Celle and had found rich pickings among the tall grass that had been allowed to flourish unchecked behind the low ex-Luftwaffe huts where No. 505 Squadron's personnel had set up their dispersal.

It was now late afternoon and the squadron had been at readiness since the early morning in anticipation of a full-strength operation, but so far no orders had come through. The pilots lounged around the dispersal, bored and keyed up at the same time, playing cards, reading or just dozing in the sun.

Yeoman was reading a newspaper. It was a day old, dated Saturday, 28 April 1945. The banner headline told of the link-up between Russian and American troops at Torgau on the Elbe three days earlier, but not announced to the world until Friday night. There was a large photograph, clearly posed, of American GIS and baggy-trousered Russians extending hands to one another over what the caption described as a rent in a bridge over the river. Both sides looked as though they distrusted each other intensely.

It was the article underneath, however, which interested Yeoman, and it had nothing to do with Torgau. He read bits of it out loud to Tim Phelan, who sat close by with his eyes shut, answering with non-committal grunts.

'It says here,' Yeoman said, 'that Mussolini has been captured, that Hitler is dying in a Berlin shelter and that Göring has shot himself. I wonder if it's true?'

Phelan gave a derisive snort. 'Don't you believe it,' he said. 'It might be true about Mussolini, but you can bet your life that old Adolf and his sidekick are sitting snug in some little bolt-hole or other, just waiting for a chance to sneak away. They won't give up that easily.'

Yeoman turned the page to read the editorial, and chuckled suddenly.

'Listen to this.' He read out a paragraph. ' "Göring — once thought a picturesque character — was a deadly menace. Drug fiend, sex pervert and sadist, he epitomized the rottenness that made Nazism the loathsome thing the whole world now knows it to be. Not since Caligula has so degraded a being wielded comparable power." '

'Wow,' Phelan grinned, 'sounds just like a couple of wing commanders I know. Poor old Hermann — they're really giving him the big hammer.' He frowned suddenly, sitting upright.

'I wonder if we'll ever know the real truth — about Hitler and his mates, I mean? You know — what they were really like.'

Yeoman shrugged and shook his head. 'I doubt it, Tim. I suppose if we'd lost the war, the Huns would have been writing much the same thing about Churchill. Propaganda is a funny thing; it often replaces truth. Remember Macbeth,' he added darkly.

Phelan looked perplexed. 'Macbeth? What the hell has he to do with anything? Don't tell me he was a Nazi too!'

'No, but he was definitely the victim of propaganda. He was really a pretty wise and just king who ruled Scotland for twenty years and stopped the Vikings kicking hell out of the place. But Malcolm, who overthrew him with English help, spread the quite untrue story that he was a foul usurper, steeped in the blood of the innocent, and all that sort of thing, Shakespeare got hold of the propaganda version and turned it into a play, and in the eyes of the world Macbeth has been a bad lad ever since.'

Phelan looked at him with respect. 'God, George, you're an educated bastard, and no mistake. You must eat history books for breakfast.'

The clamour of a telephone in the dispersal hut behind them interrupted their conversation. A moment later, a corporal stuck his head out of the window and passed the receiver to Yeoman.

'For you, sir. Group Central Control.'

Yeoman held a brief conversation with whoever was on the other end of the line and then handed the telephone back through the window before turning to his expectant pilots.

'Right, lads, we're off.' His Yorkshire accent invariably crept in slightly at moments such as these. 'Here's the gen. Offensive patrol in the Lübeck area with twelve aircraft. The main target is the Hun airfield at Schwerin, where our reconnaissance chaps have spotted a concentration of enemy fighters — including some jets. We think they might be planning to evacuate them to Denmark, and our job is to stop them. Take-off is at once.'

He grinned and clapped Tim Phelan on the back as they headed for their aircraft.

'It looks as if we might have a crack at the Luftwaffe after all. Let's hope the Russians haven't got at them first.'

*

The Meteors sped north-eastwards at ten thousand feet, in three flights of four.

As they flew on over the Elbe a thin layer of broken cloud began to spread beneath them, spreading dappled shadows over the earth far below. The Meteors cruised at the economical speed of 240 knots; if they ran into trouble, Yeoman wanted to be certain that they had sufficient fuel reserves for at least ten minutes combat.

Schwerin was not difficult to find. The town itself stood on a small peninsula that jutted out into a lake. The whole area, in fact, was a mass of lakes, surrounded by pine trees through which roads wound haphazardly. To the west of the town lay the airfield; it was one of Hitler's pre-war constructions, with a set of fine runways and a cluster of big hangars and other buildings set along one edge.

Yeoman turned the formation slightly and led it past the airfield to the south, taking a good look at what was happening on the ground. The reconnaissance boys had been right; about forty or fifty aircraft were scattered around the field. At this distance it was impossible to identify them, but from their size Yeoman decided that they must be single-seat fighters.

Yeoman detached four Meteors to remain south of the airfield, on the look-out for any enemy machines that were already airborne, and ordered the remainder into starboard echelon. As though held together by an invisible thread, the eight jets went into a steep dive towards the airfield, levelling out over the southern perimeter.

The needle on the airspeed indicator showed 430 knots as the Meteors flashed across the hangars, only feet above the grass. Yeoman had a brief glimpse of a truck, packed with soldiers, moving slowly round the perimeter track; the soldiers were waving, mistaking the Meteors for Messerschmitt 262s.

Yeoman, with Phil Trussler on his right, streaked towards a group of half a dozen Focke-Wulf 190s which were moving along one of the secondary runways in line astern, their propellers churning. He opened fire and was right on target with his first burst, seeing his shells dance and sparkle over the dark camouflage of the middle fighter. It collapsed in a cloud of dust and smoke and the one behind slammed into the wreckage, which immediately caught fire. Exploding ammunition sprayed in all directions and Yeoman ducked instinctively as the Meteor swept through the fiery smoke.

Now, for the first time, the flak opened up as the gunners realized that the speeding jets were hostile. The entire airfield lit up with flashes from guns of every calibre, firing from every angle. The single-, double-and quadruple-barrelled guns were mounted on the hangars, on top of the flat-roofed control tower and even on platforms rising above the treetops around the airfield perimeter.

Yeoman curled himself up into a ball in the cockpit, coaxing the Meteor down another few feet, and headed straight for the control tower. He pressed the firing-button and his shells 'walked' up the wall of the building, shattering the glass windows on the upper storey into powdered fragments. The twin-barrelled anti-aircraft gun on top was firing straight down his throat, the glowing shells streaming over his wings and cockpit.

Then his own shells found the gun, which disappeared in a cloud of smoke. Everything seemed to happen in slow motion. A man fell from the roof, his arms and legs flailing wildly, and disappeared from view.

Something struck the Meteor a shuddering blow. Desperately, Yeoman pulled back the stick and took the fighter over the shattered roof of the control tower with inches to spare, his port wingtip collecting several yards of a long aerial which, slung between two slender masts, he had not seen.

Heavy flak was bursting all around him, great bags of soot staining the sky. Sweating with fear, he kept the Meteor in a fast climb until the airfield was a good five miles astern, then turned to look back.

The sky over the field was a mass of drifting smoke-puffs, forming an almost solid roof through which it was hard to see anything. Several objects, including the Focke-Wulfs he had attacked, were burning on the ground. As he watched, a great pillar of flame leaped into the air from one corner of the field, where someone's cannon shells had found a fuel bowser.

Miraculously, all eight Meteors had come through the attack more or less in one piece. Two of the pilots reported that they had been hit by shell fragments, but that the damage to their aircraft was not serious.

A moment later, the leader of the four Meteors which Yeoman had detached as top cover called up the leader over the R/T.

'Good show, Ramrod Leader. That looked very pretty. Shall we attack now?'

'Negative!' Yeoman's reply was urgent; with the flak gunners fully on the alert, any aircraft making a strafing run over Schwerin now would not stand a cat in hell's chance of coming through. Instead, Yeoman ordered a pair of the Meteors to escort the two damaged aircraft back to Celle, while the remainder continued their patrol towards the north in the direction of Lübeck Bay.

The eight remaining Meteors climbed to fifteen thousand feet and crossed the north German cost near Wismar. Looking down, Yeoman could see a large concentration of shipping in Lübeck Bay and an air strike seemed to be in progress, for some of the vessels were in flames. Focusing his gaze, he made out a number of tiny crosses that were the darting silhouettes of aircraft, wheeling and turning over the coast.

Intrigued, he called up GCC and asked the fighter controller what was going on. He was told that an enemy convoy, which had been attempting to ferry reinforcements into the Lübeck sector, was under attack by a mixed force of torpedo-carrying Beaufighters and rocket-firing Typhoons. The Meteors, he was ordered, were to steer well clear.

It was a wise decision, for in the general *mêlée* the twin-engined jets would almost certainly have been mistaken for enemy aircraft, with potentially disastrous consequences. Also, the Meteors were by no means suited to tight-turning combats at treetop level.

Reluctantly, Yeoman turned his formation south again, heading inland and descending slowly. Behind them, the smoke from the burning vessels spread in a great swathe across the sky.

Suddenly, as they crossed the northern tip of the long lake that ran parallel to the Elbe-Trave Canal near Grossgronau, Phil Trussler's excited voice came over the radio.

'Aircraft, nine o'clock low — looks like a Hun!'

Yeoman looked down, and had no difficulty in locating the silvery machine. It was descending towards an expanse of pine forest, as though its pilot intended to touch down among the trees — which was exactly, Yeoman realized, what he was about to do, for a moment later he spotted a stretch of autobahn, slicing through the forest from east to west. He made a mental note to inform Intelligence of the location, then pressed the R/T button.

'All right, Phil, go and get him. But watch your step!'

Trussler acknowledged, then peeled off and went down like an arrow after the strange aircraft. Its pilot did not appear to have seen him, for he took no evasive action at all.

As he drew closer, Trussler felt excitement surge up inside him. The enemy aircraft was a jet — and a weird-looking bird at that. Very small, with short, stubby wings, it had twin tailfins and what appeared to be a single engine, mounted in a pod on top of the fuselage. Searching his memory quickly as he curved down to the attack, Trussler could not recall having seen such a type in any of the aircraft recognition material that Freddie Barnes, the Intelligence Officer, had assembled.

The curious aircraft had its wheels and flaps extended. Detachedly, Trussler noticed that it had a tricycle undercarriage.

The German drifted into the luminous diamonds of his gunsight and he opened fire at three hundred yards' range. It was a simple, no-deflection shot and a one-second burst was enough. Through his windscreen, Trussler saw the German's tail unit disintegrate. With awful finality, the aircraft's nose dropped and it plunged into the edge of the pine forest, where it exploded with a brilliant flash.

Trussler pulled up hard over the trees and went into a climbing turn, half expecting a storm of flak to pursue him, but there was none. A couple of minutes later he rejoined the other Meteors, which had been circling overhead.

'Well done, Phil,' Yeoman congratulated him. 'What was it?'

'Couldn't say, boss,' the young pilot replied. 'It was a jet job of some sort, but a really odd-looking type.'

The first thing Yeoman did on returning to Celle, after de-briefing, was to check on the identity of the mysterious aircraft. Freddie Barnes was quite sure, from the description, what type it had been.

'I'm certain it was a Heinkel 162,' he told the wing commander. There's been a lot of enemy propaganda about it lately — the Huns call it the 'Volksjäger', or people's fighter. It's thought to be in mass production, but until today I don't think any have been encountered operationally. Trussler's cine film ought to be interesting.'

As it turned out, a Heinkel 162 had already been destroyed a couple of weeks earlier in the Bremen area, so Trussler's triumph was somewhat dampened. Nevertheless, a check with Group HQ confirmed what Yeoman already suspected: Trussler had become the first Meteor pilot to destroy an enemy machine in the air. Even though the fight had been more than a little one-sided, it was excuse enough for a celebration.

The party in the mess at Celle that night was joined by a jubilant throng of Spitfire pilots. The three squadrons of the Spitfire Wing that shared Celle with the Meteors were equipped with the latest Mk XIVs, which had Rolls-Royce Griffon engines instead of the older Merlins, and they were proving more than a match for the Luftwaffe's latest piston-engined types. They had been flying almost continuously that day, providing air cover for the shipping strikes off Lübeck, and between them they had bagged twenty Messerschmitts and Focke-Wulfs in the air and on the ground. With only one day of April still left, and ninety-five aircraft destroyed in the course of the month, they were laying good-natured bets as to whether they would score five more victories during the next day's operations, bringing the total to one hundred. They claimed that no other RAF Wing had destroyed that many enemy aircraft in a single month so far, and Yeoman had no reason to doubt them.

At 2100 hours, British time, by which point everyone was feeling a little unsteady, Group Captain Kingston roared for silence and switched on the wireless. An air of expectancy fell over the bar as they all waited for the cultured tones of the BBC newsreader. It was as though, subconsciously, they were all willing him to tell them that the war was over, that there would be no more dawn take-offs, no more flak and fighters and crippled aircraft falling like stones from a tortured sky.

'The Third Reich, planned by Hitler to endure for a thousand years, is toppling now on the abyss of final destruction. It is going to its doom in a welter of rumoured revolution, of total surrender feelers and of reported assassination of the men who led it through years of battle to its end.

'The world tonight waits expectantly and tensely for the end, as message after message, flashing over cables and wireless waves, points to the swift and complete dissolution of the remnants of the shattered Nazi empire.

'It is reported that, early today, an offer of unconditional surrender to Britain and the United States — but not Russia -was made by Heinrich Himmler. Reaction in both London and Washington has been swift; only unconditional surrender to all the Allies is acceptable.'

Yeoman only half-listened to the rest of the news, vaguely hearing the announcer state that the us Seventh Army had taken Augsburg and reached the Austrian border and that the Allies were making progress in Italy, where the British Eighth Army had reached Venice. Thoughtfully, he turned to Wing Commander Liam Doyle, the tall, rangy Australian who commanded the Spitfire Wing.

'Your boys might not get a chance to bag their hundreth Hun, Liam. It looks as though it might be all over by this time tomorrow.'

Doyle shook his head. 'Don't reckon so, George. If I know the Huns they'll go on flying and fighting as long as they've got fuel and ammunition, and we might even have trouble persuading a few of 'em to surrender'.

He looked around at the throng of eager faces, shrouded in a haze of tobacco smoke. Something akin to sadness fleeted across his eyes.

'You know something, George? I'm going to miss all this. My old man's got a big sheep spread and he wants me out of the Air Force to help run the place as soon as the shooting's over, but somehow I don't fancy it. I guess maybe I'll stay in, although it'll probably mean he'll cut me off without a penny. There's more to life than being a wealthy farmer, though. What do you say?'

'Liam,' his companion replied, 'just remember one thing. Money might not bring happiness, but it certainly helps you to be miserable in comfort. Get the hell out of it, and into that nice secure job with your old man. I would, if I were in your shoes.'

Doyle peered at him through a semi-alcoholic haze and his mouth twisted into a cynical smile.

'George,' he said, jabbing the other's chest with an index finger, 'you're a hell of a nice guy and I like you a lot. But you're an awful bloody liar!'

Chapter Nine

BEFORE THE WAR, BERLIN'S SUBWAY SYSTEM HAD BEEN ONE OF the finest in the world. Now it was a labyrinthine hell, an underground battlefield where the living were mingled inextricably with the dead.

The Germans, retreating on the city centre, had set up command posts in the tunnels under Berlin's main railway stations, which now resembled armed camps. Women and children huddled in every niche and corner, their eyes wild with terror, listening to the continual roar of approaching battle. Every so often, the improvized shelters shook with fearful concussions as shells exploded in the streets above, showering cement from the roofs.

Inevitably, there was panic. People fought each other like wild animals around the ladders that ran up the air shafts into the streets. Worse was to come; on Hitler's orders, engineers blew the bulkheads that separated a section of the tunnels from the Landwehr Canal, releasing a flood of water that turned the tunnels into a shrieking nightmare as crowds tore at one another in their desperate efforts to escape, stumbling and falling over rails and sleepers, abandoning their wailing children in their mindless flight.

Trampled bodies lay on the tracks. The waters rose and the corpses drifted on them. Even when the flood subsided, the panic persisted.

Elsewhere in the subways, men, women and children burned alive in screaming agony as Russian shock troops blasted their way towards the city centre with flame-throwers, fighting their way through the tunnels in the hope of emerging behind the German positions. There was no longer any semblance of cohesion; scattered units, cut off from one another, fought and died or surrendered where they stood.

The troops of the 'Müncheberg' Division had retreated steadily north-westwards to the Potsdamer Station, just round the corner from the Reich Chancellery. The station's main entrance was a sickening sight; a Russian shell had exploded in the corridor and the remains of men, women and children were literally plastered around the walls. Outside, the Potsdamerplatz was littered with smashed vehicles, ambulances with the wounded still lying in them, and corpses, many of them fearfully mangled by tank tracks. Desperate medical officers hammered on cellar doors and begged civilians who were sheltering there to take some of the wounded in; mostly the civilians refused, fearful that they would be tried and executed by the roving ss squads as 'accomplices in desertion'.

For the fighting troops, there was no rest, no relief, and hardly any food. For drinking, they obtained water from the tunnels — water stained with human blood and every imaginable kind of filth — and filtered it as best they could.

Yet even now, wild rumours persisted that Berlin was about to be saved by a miracle. It was said that a separate armistice had been signed with the western Allies, and that even now General Wenck's column was marching to the relief of the city with the support of several American divisions.

Wenck had in fact launched his attack at dawn on 28 April, his xx Corps consisting of three divisions made up of men from the officer-training schools. They were the elite of the German Army and they struck hard and fast, covering fifteen miles by the afternoon to a point south-west of Potsdam; but their flanks were unprotected, and in the Lehnin Forest, through which the advance speared, the hardened troops of the Russian 4th Guards Tank Army quickly recovered from their initial surprise and began to fight back.

Wenck's assault enabled the surrounded garrison at Potsdam to make their escape, but Berlin itself was still twenty miles away and to continue the advance would have been nothing short of suicide. That night, on the authorization of Feldmarschall Keitel, Wenck accordingly turned round and marched his thirty thousand men towards the west, where in due course he would surrender his command more or less intact to the Americans.

Slowly but inexorably, the defenders of Berlin were being forced back on all sides to make what would be their last stand around the Chancellery, under which several hundred people still lived a troglodyte existence in the labyrinth of bunkers. This underground ant's nest was a masterpiece of design and planning, each of the concrete shelters a little world of its own with lighting and oxygen supply, sleeping quarters, kitchens, guard rooms and dining rooms, and each linked by lateral galleries to each other and to the hub of the whole complex, the Führerbunker itself.

Of the Nazi hierarchy, only the faithful Goebbels and Martin Bormann, the Party Secretary, remained with their leader now. The other occupants of the various bunkers, soldiers and civilians alike, were little more than relics of the great administration that had ruled Europe — all but one small, defiant island — for five bloody years. Some were there, under the ruins of Berlin, because it was their natural post and they had nowhere else to go; others, like Richter and von Gleiwitz, because fate had swept them there to be caught up unwillingly in the great city's death throes.

They were oblivious to the horror above them; even when a shell exploded close by, the ground trembled and the ventilators admitted a hot breath of dust and fumes, it was a happening as remote as the moon, its reality dulled by the constant muted roar of the complex's diesel-driven generators. In the bunkers, the awful reality of the world outside no longer existed.

Hanna Reitsch and Ritter von Greim left the bunker on the night of the twenty-eighth and flew to safety in a battered old Arado training aircraft, which a Luftwaffe sergeant — the same man who had flown them into Gatow — had risked his life to bring in. Before he departed, von Greim had shaken hands with both Richter and von Gleiwitz and had looked at them with eyes which were sad and almost apologetic, as though to convey the unspoken message that he would gladly have taken both men with him, had there been enough room.

Apart from organizing air support for a last, impossible German offensive, Ritter von Greim had been given another task: to arrest SS Reichsführer Heinrich Himmler for treason. A few hours earlier, Hitler had learned of Himmler's efforts to negotiate an armistice with the British and Americans through Count Bernadotte, the Swiss Red Cross representative.

It was the last straw. Hitler had never dreamed that the man he had dubbed 'Faithful Heinrich' — the man responsible for the callous murder of millions of innocent people — would desert him in the final hours. The Führer's bitterness and self-pity brimmed over. In the early hours of the morning, he ordered Martin Bormann to send a signal to Grand

Admiral Donitz, who, at his headquarters in the Schleswig-Holstein town of Flensburg near the Danish border, was now Hitler's deputy:

'The foreign press reports fresh treason. The Führer expects that you will act with lightning speed and iron severity against all traitors in the north German area. Without exception, Schorner, Wenck and the others must give evidence of their loyalty by the quickest relief of the Führer.'

Even as the signal was being despatched, Hitler was considering a breakout plan brought to him by General Weidling, who commanded the final defence of Berlin. Wearily, the Führer rejected it; it would, he declared, be better to face his end where he was, rather than 'in some farmhouse or under the open sky'.

Another signal followed the earlier one to Admiral Donitz. It spelled out the death warrant for many in the bunker complex. It said simply:

'We will hold out to the end.'

Outside, the panic was reaching its climax. Hundreds of soldiers of the Berlin garrison had begun to desert; those who were caught were either shot on the spot or hanged from the nearest tree, stripped of their uniforms, the placards round their necks bearing the words: WE BETRAYED THE FÜHRER!

The SS execution squads descended on the underground stations. Anyone whose face they did not like they hauled outside and shot. Soldier or civilian, it made no difference. In some cases, they herded all the men outside and gave them rifles, pointing them in the direction of the fighting. Anyone who hesitated received a bullet through the head.

This was the cause to which Richter, von Gleiwitz and all the other idealistic young men had given their allegiance, and fought, and died.

The centre of Berlin was now defended by wild, fanatical men who had nothing to lose; men such as the remnants of the Vlassov Division, Russians from the Ukraine and elsewhere, who greeted the German invaders as liberators in 1941 and who could expect no mercy if they were taken alive. Men such as the French and Belgian Waffen SS, who had been bitter opponents of the rise of communism in their countries before the war and who had seen, in Hitler, a kind of avenging angel who would impose the iron grip of a fascist regime upon the world; now they, together with Hitler's own SS and the more fanatical elements of the Hitler youth, were selling their lives dearly at every street corner, behind every mound of rubble.

Incredibly, amid all the bombing and shelling and machine-gun fire, civilian life of sorts went on. The bread queues started at three o'clock in the morning, when the streets near bakers' shops filled with long snakes of grey, starving people, many of them grotesquely adorned with steel helmets. The queues persisted, even when shellfire raked the streets and low-flying Russian aircraft swooped down with their machine-guns blazing, taking a fearful toll.

Often, the sacrifices were in vain, for there was enough bread to supply only a fraction of the people in the queues. It was then that the real panic began, for fear of slow starvation — and the tragedy of returning empty-handed to crying children who had been hungry for days — was greater by far than any fear of death from shrapnel or bullets.

A rumour that some sausages were available in a market hall produced a wild stampede in which dozens were trampled to death or died, simply, because their weakened hearts gave out. Hundreds of women crammed their way into the hall, clawing at one another to get closer to the long counter. A salvo of heavy-calibre Russian shells smashed through the roof and exploded among them, tearing them to pieces. Rescue squads dragged out the mutilated bodies of the dead and piled them on to carts along with the wounded; those who had escaped unharmed went on waiting, pushing steadily forward towards the counter through the blood and human fragments that littered the ground ...

In the bunker, Hitler had married Eva Braun. She had remained with her god, faithful and adoring, until the very end, echoing the curses of heaven and hell which he rained down on those he believed to have betrayed him.

Not even Breughel, in all his visions of the inferno, could have envisaged such a bizarre scene as that attending Hitler's wedding feast; the sullen bridegroom, waiting only for the inevitable end but afraid to face it; the silent guests, with dust wafted in from outside floating on their champagne; Eva Braun, happy, a vacant smile on her face, yet knowing that outside the door of the bunker lay the body of her brother-in-law, Hermann Fegelein, accused of treachery and executed only minutes earlier on Hitler's orders ...

Richter and von Gleiwitz, who had confined themselves to the communications centre in the Second SS Bunker, drank a cynical toast to the Führer's health. Not far away, in the canteen, dozens of SS men and women 'auxiliary helpers' were hopelessly drunk; they had been like that for days, playing American jazz music over and over again, dancing, copulating in dark corners.

Along with everyone else in the bunker, the two Luftwaffe officers were playing a waiting game — but one of a different kind. Confusion and chaos were their allies. So they waited, and listened, and watched, and stayed as inconspicuous as possible while the crazy world around them collapsed stone by stone.

In the early hours of the twenty-ninth Hitler made his will and dictated some final political instructions, among which he named Admiral Donitz as his successor and authorized him to assume the title President of the Reich. Goebbels was to be the new Reichs Chancellor, and Martin Bormann Party Minister in Donitz's cabinet.

It was nothing more than a farce, a pretence that some machinery of government still existed in the ruins of Germany. The life of the Third Reich was measured now in hours, and nothing could save the phantoms in the bunker — not even the heroic efforts of a handful of Luftwaffe crews, who on the night of the 28/29 April had braved murderous flak and Russian night fighters to drop supplies into the Berlin Pocket. Four aircraft had flown the mission from an airfield in Schleswig-Holstein; two had returned, and most of the supplies had fallen into Russian hands.

There would be no more air supply missions. General Weidling reported the fact personally to Hitler, and also told him that the shrinking ring of defenders around the Chancellery had ammunition for only another twenty-four hours, perhaps less.

Shortly before midnight on the twenty-ninth Hitler drafted his last signal. It consisted of five questions, to which his closest advisers already knew the answers. Where were Wenck's spearheads? When would they attack again? Where was the 9th Army? Where was it breaking through? Where were the 41st Panzer Corps spearheads?

And the answers, drafted by Feldmarschall Keitel, formed Berlin's epitaph. Wenck's point had come to a halt south of Schwielow Lake, and the whole of his eastern flank was under strong Soviet attack. As a consequence, 12th Army was unable to continue its offensive towards Berlin. The 9th Army was encircled; a single Panzer group had succeeded in breaking out towards the west, but its location was unknown. The 41st Panzer Corps was on the defensive.

Minutes after Keitel's signal was received, the transmitter balloon that floated over the Tiergarten was shot down by Russian artillery fire.

In the bunker complex they waited, sleepless and red-eyed. Outside, a bloody sun rose through the dust and smoke to greet the last day of April. Still they waited, shaken by the continual crash of shellfire.

Shortly before noon, a squad of Waffen SS arrived at the Chancellery and took delivery of a letter from Hitler to General Weidling. Its wording was a reprieve for several hundred men.

'To the commander of the Berlin Defence District, Artillery General Weidling: in the event of the defenders of the Reich Capital running out of ammunition and supplies, I give my authority to break out. Defenders are to break out in small groups and attempt to join up with troops who are still fighting. If this is not possible, small groups are to continue the fight in the woods. Adolf Hitler.'

Richter and von Gleiwitz were alone in the communications centre when, shortly after half-past three that afternoon, an SS Sturmführer burst in through the door. Swaying and ashen-faced, he leaned against the wall for support and stared at the •two men with glazed eyes. He swallowed several times, and then said in a voice hoarse with emotion:

'It is finished. Our Führer has shot himself. Frau Hitler is dead also.'

The man collapsed into a chair and covered his face with his hands, breaking into racking sobs. Then a shudder ran through him and his emotional spasm passed. He rose slowly to his feet, and Richter saw with horror that there was madness in his eyes.

'Brave comrades!' the Sturmführer cried. 'Follow me! We shall join the Führer and return with the legions of hell to sweep the curse of Bolshevism from the earth!'

In a single, fluid movement, he drew his pistol, rammed the muzzle into his mouth and pulled the trigger. His brains splattered messily on the wall behind him.

The two Luftwaffe officers stared at the body in silence for a few moments. Then Richter faced his adjutant and said:

'Tonight, Hasso. We must go tonight, as soon as it's dark. Just the two of us. If we join up with any of those lunatics, it'll be suicide. There's still a corridor open through the city centre at least as far as the Havel. That's our lifeline.'

'We don't stand a chance,' von Gleiwitz said hopelessly. 'Even if we get as far as the Havel, the country beyond must be stiff with Russians. How are we going to get past them — fly?'

Richter smiled, 'Precisely, Hasso. I think it's time I showed you my trump card.'

He reached into his pocket and wordlessly handed von Gleiwitz a piece of paper. It was a page from a signal message pad, with a few words scrawled on it.

'I was on duty here alone when this signal arrived just a few hours ago,' Richter explained. 'I thought it prudent to keep it to myself-you'll see why.'

Von Gleiwitz looked at the wording, and his eyes widened in surprise. 'My God, Jo,' he said, forgetting their difference in rank, 'you took a hell of a risk!'

The signal was from Admiral Donitz's HQ, and read: 'At approximately 0400 hours on 1 May a flying-boat will attempt a landing on Lake Havel with the object of evacuating the Führer and his personal staff. Aircraft will remain on Havel for thirty minutes only. Accurate timing for escape attempt is imperative.'

New hope dawned in von Gleiwitz's face as he handed the paper back to Richter.

'Do you think it will still come, sir?'

'It will come, Hasso,' Richter assured him. 'Those fellows in Flensburg do not yet know that Hitler is dead. And when it leaves Berlin, you and I are going to be on it.'

Chapter Ten

THE BLOHM UND VOSS BVI38 FLYING-BOAT CHURNED ITS WAY across the darkened waters of the Isefjord, north of Copenhagen, and lifted into the air, heading along the Danish coast.

At the controls, Major Walter Kleber felt slightly sick; not from the turbulence that rocked the aircraft, but from the thought of what lay ahead of him. The fact that he had been ordered to undertake this mission, he supposed, was the penalty he had to pay for being the most experienced pilot in the Luftwaffe's 299th Long-Range Maritime Reconnaissance Squadron, veteran of many flights over the ocean from Britain's western Atlantic approaches to Norway's North Cape. Many of his comrades had failed to return from those latter missions, their bodies lost forever in the freezing waters beyond the Arctic Circle.

It was exactly 0200 hours on Tuesday, 1 May, and nothing seemed worth dying for any more — not even the orders he carried in his tunic pocket, with all the awesome responsibility they settled on his shoulders. But orders of any kind had to be carried out; Kleber's oath of allegiance to the Reich and the Führer still held good.

His task looked simple enough on the face of it. Admittedly, it called for a landing on the outskirts of Berlin, under the muzzles of Russian guns, with hardly anything in the way of navigational aids; there were not even any charts and Kleber had briefed his crew that night with the aid of a map of northern Germany torn out of a school atlas.

The BV138 crossed the north German coast near Warnemünde at less than a thousand feet, keeping low to avoid detection by prowling Russian night fighters. Away in the distance the crew could vaguely make out the town of Wittenberge; there, Allied forces were forging a bridgehead across the Elbe, and the sky was lit up by flashes of artillery fire.

As they approached Berlin, the crew gazed in horror at the scene that unfolded beneath them. The whole earth seemed to be in flames, and the sky above the outskirts of the city itself was thick with sparks and ashes. The cockpit filled with smoke, permeated with a sickly stench of decay. Berlin, which had once been one of the most beautiful cities in Europe, was now a huge furnace, the rivers of fire that ran through its shattered streets punctuated by the sudden vivid flashes of shellbursts as Russian guns pounded the last pockets of German resistance.

The flying boat droned on past the shattered city, turning in from the south. Over the southern outskirts the sky suddenly erupted in a whirlwind of anti-aircraft fire and probing searchlights stabbed upwards, threatening to ensnare the machine in a web of light. Sweating with fear and half blinded by the searchlights and the glare of burning buildings, the pilot took the BV138 down in a screaming dive almost to ground level, racing along the line of the River Havel in a northerly direction.

Kleber strained his eyes ahead, trying to pick out landmarks, but in all this holocaust of flame and smoke it was difficult to distinguish anything. All he could do was follow the river and hope for the best. Then, suddenly, a strange and almost terrifying sight materialized ahead and slightly off to starboard. It looked for all the world like a glistening patch of blood, emerging from the lurid darkness. Kleber breathed a sigh of relief as he recognized it for what it was — one of the lakes on the river, its flat surface reflecting the fires of the dying city.

There was a darker patch in the middle of the red and Kleber identified it immediately as Pfauen Island, with the broad inlet of the Wannsee beyond it on the left. A little further on, a promontory jutted out into the broad expanse of river; their designated landing area was just on the other side, where the east bank was reported to be still in German hands.

Praying that the report was true, Kleber brought the BV138 in for a straight approach, sweeping across the promontory and flattening out over the lurid water. The flying boat's hull made contact but the speed was too high and the big machine bounced back into the air again, hanging helplessly for long seconds before splashing down for good and churning across the lake in a great wake of foam.

Kleber closed the throttles, bringing the BVI38's three engines to idling rpm, and peered out into the darkness, searching the east bank of the river for some form of signal. He had been told to expect a flashing light, repeating a coded combination of letters, but there was nothing. Surely, he thought, someone must have seen the big aircraft touch down. Fear welled up inside him at the thought that something might have gone terribly wrong.

Suddenly, the whole scene became as bright as day. From the west bank, parachute flares arced up into the sky and burst over the river, flooding the area with their stark, pitiless light. Seconds later, streams of tracer reached out, groping for the flying boat. Machine-gun bullets chattered around it and cannon shells erupted alongside, raising fountains of water. In the light of the flares, Kleber could now see dark, humped shapes on the west bank of the river. They were Russian tanks, and they were blazing away at him with all their guns.

It was impossible for the Russians to miss. The flying boat shuddered as bullets and splinters smashed into it. Kleber's flight engineer screamed and collapsed at his position, his back door open by a fragment of white-hot metal. Kleber himself felt a stinging whiplash blow on his cheek; he touched the spot and his hand came away bloody, but he thankfully realized that the wound was not serious.

He opened the throttles and the flying boat surged forward, turning away from the danger and ordering the crew to fire back. The thud of the 20-mm cannon in the rear turret was joined by the lighter clatter of a single 7.9-mm machine gun. It was a futile gesture, for none of the aircraft's armament could hope to make any impression on the T-34s, but it kept the crew from panicking while the pilot taxied for the shadowy east bank.

Zig-zagging furiously as he taxied, Kleber brought the BV I 38 round the end of the promontory north of the Wannsee. The Russian fire slowly died away as the parachute flares fizzled out and the aircraft was lost to sight among the shadows. Kleber, sweating and trembling with reaction, closed down the engines and allowed the aircraft to drift in an eerie silence.

*

The breakout from the Chancellery bunker, which both Richter and von Gleiwitz had both been secretly dreading for fear of being shot by their own side, had in the event proved almost ridiculously easy. The SS guards had melted away, and small groups of personnel had begun to make their escape from the bunker complex as soon as darkness fell on 30 April.

In the Chancellery garden, the bodies of Adolf Hitler and Eva Braun lay unrecognizably charred in a shell hole under a mound of earth, their grave unmarked, the SS guards having tried and failed to obliterate them completely with burning gasoline. In the Führerbunker, Goebbels was preparing himself and his family for death, while Martin Bormann — faithful only to himself, as he had always been — was making ready to save his own skin. As yet, the world outside the bunker did not know that Hitler was dead.

The great flak towers in the Tiergarten were still firing, using the remainder of their ammunition on the Russian armoured columns that were closing in on the city centre. In the Frankfurter Allee, the road was blocked by Soviet tanks, shattered by the guns' 120-mm shells. To the north-east, another quadruple flak tower above the Friedrichshain bunker was also holding out in an isolated island, shattered and scarred by enemy artillery but still pumping shells at the Russians advancing southwards along the Chausseestrasse.

Before leaving the bunker, the two Luftwaffe officers had made a careful study of the known German positions. On the other side of the Tiergarten the Russians had captured the Reichstag after a bitter fight and the red flag now fluttered over the ruins, but westwards from the Chancellery a narrow corridor was still open, running through Charlottenburg to the suburbs. The corridor was nowhere more than half a mile wide and was under terrific Russian fire, but it was being fiercely defended and was likely to remain open for another few hours at least. Whether the corridor extended as far as the Havel Richter had no idea, but everything depended on it; if the Russians were on the east bank, it was certain that any flying boat attempting to land on the river would be destroyed.

Equipped with steel helmets and machine-pistols — a precaution Richter considered necessary, for if they were stopped by an SS patrol they could pretend that they were on their way to the front line, and Richter still had General Christian's order in his pocket authorizing them to move freely around what was left of the German-held part of the city — they emerged from the bunker after nightfall into clouds of choking, reddish smoke. It was the first time either of them had been out of the bunker for three days, and at first they had difficulty in getting their bearings. They were surrounded by a featureless wilderness of rubble, and the drifting smoke made it impossible to see more than a few metres in any direction. Then a sudden rift in the smoke revealed the shattered trees of the Tiergarten ahead of them, stark in the lurid glare of flames, and they headed in that direction, running from crater to crater as shells crashed around them.

They went at a run down the Bellevue Allee, dodging mounds of wreckage, retching involuntarily as the acrid smoke seized their throats. All around them, in the miniature lakes that wound through the zoological gardens, dead animals floated. The Tiergarten was a place of dead things, the animals that the children of Berlin had once flocked to see shot by squads of soldiers to put them out of their misery.

Other figures moved through the smoke like phantoms, but no one took any notice of the two men in the deafening rain of shellfire, the thudding of mortars and the bark of weapons of every kind. Their flight was a nightmare progression from one stinking shell-hole to the next, their uniforms stained with filth and slime.

Once, as they entered the Berlinstrasse, they threw themselves down in fear under the smouldering wreck of a tram as a group of men came running towards them out of the murk, shouting in a foreign language; but the language was French, and Richter realized that the men must belong to the French storm-battalion of the 'Charlemagne' volunteer division, whose men had been fighting like demons in the capital. A few days earlier, Richter had been present when Hitler had presented one of them with the Iron Cross for knocking out five Russian tanks single-handed with a Panzerfaust rocket launcher.

Nevertheless, Richter and von Gleiwitz stayed hidden until after the troops had passed. French they might be, but they were still ss, and they were imbued with the fanaticism of men who faced inevitable death. It was ironic, Richter thought as they struggled on through the rubble, that the final defence of Berlin should lie in the hands of foreigners after so many of the German garrison had fled; men like those holding the perimeter that was shrinking rapidly around the Tiergarten, Dutchmen, Belgians, Danes and Letts of the 'Nordland' SS Volunteer Panzer Grenadier Division, fighting alongside the Germans of the 18th Panzer Grenadier Division. Somehow, it made Richter feel guilty to be fleeing, but he quickly found reassurance in the thought that thousands of his fellow-countrymen were doing exactly the same thing.

The two men pushed on, metre after aching metre, keeping close to the shadows around the ruins wherever possible. The noise of battle all around them had become a kind of dull silence, like the roar of an aircraft engine when one has spent several hours sitting behind it. The Russian shelling had died away considerably, presumably because the Russian gunners were now afraid of hitting their own troops, but the odd shell still came screeching over to explode with a sharp crack among the shattered buildings that flanked the street, causing the fugitives to flatten themselves among the splintered glass and smashed stone that lay everywhere.

Not only concrete and glass littered the streets. There were bodies everywhere, and the stench was sickening. Once, von Gleiwitz accidentally stepped on a corpse and recoiled in horror as the pent-up gases inside it escaped with an explosive noise under the pressure of his foot. Gagging, he covered his mouth with his hand and staggered away, feeling the vomit rising in his throat.

Richter grabbed him by the arm and urged him roughly on, although his own stomach was also churning with nausea. It was nearly four hours since they had left the bunker, and they still had a long way to go if they were to reach the Havel by 0400.

The smoke was thinner now, and beyond its drifting wraiths they could make out a skeletal structure of twisted metal, at one second in stark outline against some distant fire, the next almost invisible in the shadows. Richter pointed to it.

'The radio tower,' he said hoarsely, spitting out a mouthful of grit. 'The Grunewald is just beyond it. We'll really have to watch our step now — we don't know how far the Russians have penetrated.'

They could hear a lot of shooting somewhere ahead of them, but it seemed to be mostly small-arms fire and it was still a considerable way off, on the other side of the Grunewald. They set off in that direction, on the assumption that German forces must still be holding the western corridor open as far as the Havel.

Before the war — and, indeed, during much of the war — the Grunewald, or 'Green Wood', had been Berlin's principal recreation area, a vast expanse of trees, lakes and open parks. Now it was a nightmare of splintered, broken tree trunks and branches, a tangled desert spattered with bomb and shell craters.

Moving through it seemed unreal. All around, guns were barking and vivid flashes lit up the sky. The noise was hellish, yet Richter and von Gleiwitz seemed to be walking in an oasis of darkness, undisturbed by what was going on elsewhere. Only once did a German voice call to them out of the darkness; they could not tell if they were being challenged, but in any case they had melted away into the night before anyone made a move towards them.

Richter, having foreseen the problem of finding their way through a blackened city whose face had changed out of all recognition, had brought a small, luminous compass with him, and stopped from time to time in order to get his bearings. Intuitively, he had decided to cut diagonally across the Grünewald from north-east to south-west, heading in the general direction of the Wannsee. German armoured units had been holding out in that area at dawn that day, and as far as he knew the position had not changed — indeed, the noise of firing from that quarter seemed to confirm that it had not.

In a sense, Richter and von Gleiwitz had been lucky to begin their escape attempt when they did. In Berlin, orders were only just going out to the various defense pockets from General Weidling authorizing a mass break-out attempt. The firing the two Luftwaffe officers could hear came from an armoured detachment that was holding one of the bridges over the Havel near Potsdam; it was the last fragile road out of the Berlin pocket.

It was fortunate for the fugitives that the main Russian thrusts into Berlin had come from north and south, where no large waterways barred access to the city. Here, in the west, the broad expanse of the Havel formed a big natural obstacle; the Russians had by-passed it to the north, capturing the bridges over the River Spree at Spandau, between Havel Lake and the Heiligensee, but the Havel lay like a moat along the city's south-west edge and the Russians, after capturing Gatow airfield on the other side, had been content so far to set up gun batteries on the western edge of the expanse of water and from there to pound the German defences in the Grünewald.

Because the Havel was now impassable except for the single bridge which still stood at Potsdam, and which was held by the Germans, the latter had concentrated most of their available forces there, leaving only scattered outposts along the remainder of the east bank. Richter and his adjutant consequently reached the waterway unchallenged and moved cautiously along the bank towards the promontory that jutted out to the north of the Wannsee, noting as they moved that they would have little trouble in reaching the flying-boat if the latter arrived; small boats were beached all along the east bank of the Havel, having been used to ferry troops across from Gatow.

Half a mile from the promontory, the fugitives settled down under a clump of bushes to wait. Richter had already made up his mind that if the flying-boat did not turn up, they would head towards Potsdam and try and slip through the encircling Russians without waiting for the garrison's main breakout attempt. He was certain that the latter was doomed to failure, anyway.

They waited for half an hour, in an agony of suspense. Apart from sporadic shooting, the crossfire over the Havel had died away. It was in the sudden lull that they first heard the distant sound of aero-engines.

'Could be a Russian,' von Gleiwitz said gloomily. His companion shook his head in excitement.

'No, those are Junkers Jumos. I'd recognize their sound anywhere. It's a BV138, all right.'

The noise of the motors swelled, then faded towards the south.

'It's going away,' von Gleiwitz said miserably. Richter made no reply; he kept his head tilted to one side, listening.

After a few minutes they heard the aero-engines again, approaching from the south. Both men saw the aircraft at the same time, a great dark shape swooping down out of the night, silhouetted against the fires that raged in Potsdam, several miles away. The foam that creamed up from beneath its hull caught the ruddy light, spraying outwards like bloody froth.

They watched the BV138 turn towards the east bank, then drift to a stop, its propellers turning slowly. An instant later, the flares went up and a storm of fire lanced across the Havel towards the machine, which began to move again towards the shadow of the promontory, its guns spitting return fire.

'Come on!'

Richter slapped von Gleiwitz on the shoulder and the two men began to run along the bank towards the aircraft, which was now disappearing in the shadows. Gradually, the Russian fire died away.

Breathing hard, they reached a point opposite the flying-boat, which lay dimly visible a hundred metres or so from the bank. The last of the enemy flares spurted into a brief lease of life and then spluttered out, making the night seem darker than before.

Richter looked around quickly. Splintered trees lay behind them, the water in front. Firing was still in progress over to their left, beyond the promontory, but they seemed to have this part of the Havel bank to themselves.

Richter tapped von Gleiwitz on the arm and they hurried down to the water's edge, where they had earlier seen some small boats. Offshore, the dark hulk of the BV138 lay still and silent and Richter realized that the crew were waiting for someone to make contact with them.

Several of the boats were wrecked, riddled with shell splinters, but the fugitives found one that was intact and complete with oars. Placing their machine-pistols inside, they exerted their strength and began to push it towards the water.

'Halt!'

The sharp command rang through the night and Richter felt his stomach reel. He looked at von Gleiwitz and shook his head resignedly, silently warning the other not to make a grab for the weapons in the boat, then turned round slowly.

A few metres away, up the slope of the bank, three steel-helmeted men stood, their legs braced apart. All three carried Schmeissers, and the muzzles were pointing menacingly at the Luftwaffe officers.

One of the men beckoned imperiously. 'Come here! Put your hands in the air!'

Richter and his adjutant trudged slowly back up the bank and halted before the three men, their hands raised. The fitful light of the fires across the lake reflected from their helmets, and from the SS insignia on their collars.

The taller of the three, a hauptsturmführer, poked the muzzle of his gun into Richter's midriff. When he spoke, his voice was sinister and charged with menace.

'So what have we here? Two Luftwaffe officers, a colonel and a major. What are you doing here? Give an account of yourselves.'

Richter tentatively lowered an arm and pointed towards the flying-boat. 'Special orders,' he said, striving to keep his voice steady. 'We have come direct from the Führerbunker to make contact with the crew of that aircraft. I have the relevant orders here, if you will permit me to show them to you.'

The SS officer extended his hand. Richter reached into his pocket and passed the man the copy of the radio message from Flensburg, together with General Christian's movement order. The SS officer peered at them closely, tilting the papers so that the dull light of the flames fell on them. Then, with a contemptuous gesture, he crumpled them into a ball and tossed them away.

'The Führer is dead,' he said softly. 'You can't fool me, Colonel. You and your colleague here were trying to save your own skins. Isn't that it? Yes of course it is. And there is still a penalty for cowards and traitors such as you!'

He gave Richter a sudden jab in the chest that sent the Luftwaffe officer staggering backwards. As though in a nightmare, he heard the metallic clicks as the SS men cocked their Schmeissers. There was no time for anything, not even to tell von Gleiwitz that he was sorry.

He closed his eyes. A volley of shots crashed out through the night.

Chapter Eleven

RICHTER OPENED HIS EYES AGAIN. HE WAS SHAKING FROM head to foot, his bladder on the point of emptying itself. Hot and cold waves shuddered through him alternately.

The three ss men lay sprawled at his feet. One moaned and tried to rise, groping for his gun; a single shot rang out and the man jerked and kicked a few times before the life ran out of him.

Dazedly, Richter looked up. From the splintered trees, four shadowy figures advanced towards him. The leading figure carried a gun; two of the others seemed to be supporting the third. The newcomers stopped and the leader addressed Richter, who recoiled with momentary shock. The voice was a woman's. The German was faultless, but there was the trace of an accent which Richter was unable to place.

'We've been watching you,' the woman told him. 'We saw you go into hiding, and assumed from the nervous way in which you were behaving that you were trying to get away — presumably on that.' She indicated the flying-boat.

Richter neither confirmed nor denied her words. Instead, he said stiffly:

'We must thank you for saving our lives. But who are you? And who are these people?'

'That doesn't matter. What matters is that we are trying to get out of Berlin, the same as you apparently are. You can have explanations later, if you like, but not now — there isn't time. Will you take us with you?'

Von Gleiwitz spoke for the first time. His voice was still trembling slightly with reaction.

'Why are you so important?' He wanted to know. 'We are thankful that you saved our lives, but why should you have precedence over all the other civilians who are fleeing from the Russians?'

'And why, young man, should you have precedence over all your own wounded soldiers, many of whom will probably die in Russian camps if they are left behind?'

The speaker, one of the three men, shrugged off the arm of the colleague who had been supporting him and came forward to confront von Gleiwitz, limping badly. He was old and small and he craned his neck, peering intently at the Luftwaffe officer's features.

'Young man,' he ordered, 'take off your helmet!'

Like a small boy who had been ordered to stand in the corner, von Gleiwitz did as he was told. The old man peered at him even more closely.

'I thought so,' he grunted. 'The uniform almost had me fooled, Gleiwitz, but I have a better memory than you. Class of thirty-two, Heidelberg University. You were the worst student of physical science it was ever my misfortune to teach.'

Von Gleiwitz gasped in amazement as recognition dawned, 'It can't be! Professor Gorbach — in God's name, how do you come to be here?'

'It's a long story,' Gorbach said drily. 'Now then, Gleiwitz, all you need to know is that the Russians are chasing us, and that we don't want them to capture us. Now, are you going to take us with you, or not? Be quick and make up your mind — I don't think we have a great deal of time.'

Von Gleiwitz turned to Richter. 'Sir,' he said quickly, 'I think we should take them. If Professor Gorbach says the Russians are after them, it must be for some important reason. After all,' he added desperately, 'what do we stand to lose?'

Richter's mind was quickly made up for him. On the lake behind, the flying-boat was starting its engines.

On board the BV138, Major Kleber had started the engines again more as a precautionary measure than anything else. The authorized period of waiting on the lake was not yet up, but he wanted to be in a position to make a quick getaway if he was threatened. He had no idea whether the Russians had reached the east bank of the lake or not; for all he knew, they might even now be preparing to open fire on him from point-blank range. To be on the safe side, he ordered his gunners to stay alert and be on the lookout for any sign of trouble.

Suddenly, a shout of alarm came from the nose gunner. A single boat was approaching from the east bank. Kleber ordered the man to keep an eye on it, then opened the starboard hatch and leaned out precariously, his pistol in his hand, covering the approaching craft.

'Who are you?' he cried. 'Identify yourselves, or we open fire!'

The reply was instantaneous. 'Don't shoot! Colonel Richter, Reichsluftwaffe. Orders from the Führer Headquarters!'

'All right, then, come alongside. No funny business.' Despite his alarm Kleber was forced to smile at himself. He sounded like a character out of an American western film.

The boat drifted up gently and bumped against the flying boat's hull near the hatch. Kleber peered down into the little craft; it contained six people, two of whom were in uniform.

'All right. One of you only may come aboard. You, Richter. The rest of you remain exactly where you are. My gunner has orders to open fire if you make any wrong move.'

Richter clambered through the hatch and faced the pilot. Formally, he said:

'It is my duty to inform you that the Führer is dead.'

Kleber showed no sign of emotion. Then, quietly, he asked whether Richter had any proof. Richter shook his head, and rapidly outlined what he knew of the circumstances of Hitler's suicide and the disposal of his body.

Kleber nodded. 'I have no choice but to believe you, Colonel. But who, then, are the people in the boat?'

Again, Richter told him what he knew, aware that the information sounded hopelessly sketchy and inadequate. In the end, at Kleber's request, Professor Gorbach came on board and spoke quietly but with authority to the pilot, clarifying the position.

Kleber shrugged. 'The whole world's gone crazy,' he muttered. 'All right, then, get everybody on board and let's get out of here. It will be daylight soon, and if we don't get away before then I don't give a fig for our chances.'

The others clambered into the flying-boat. Kleber stared in amazement at the woman, who was still clutching her machine-pistol. He opened his mouth to ask about her, then thought better of it and turned away, giving orders for the body of the dead flight engineer to be placed in the boat. He would have preferred to fly the man back to Copenhagen for a decent burial, but was conscious of the fact that with the extra people on board, the aircraft was already close to being fully laden.

'More boats, Major! Putting out from the shore!'

The nose gunner's urgent cry sent Kleber back to the hatch. The gunner was right; a small armada of boats, all of them laden to the gunwales, was converging on the BV138. Shadowy figures were waving frantically. Kleber knew that they could only be German soldiers, desperate to escape the Russian trap. He also knew that he could not possibly take more than two or three on board.

A vision of a horde of panic-stricken soldiers trying to claw their way into the aircraft, swamping it and preventing it from taking off, flashed through his mind and the instinct of self-preservation outweighed every other consideration. He ran forward to the flight deck and literally threw himself into the pilot's seat, pushing open the throttles and sending a surge of power through the idling engines. The BV138 began to move, creaming round in a turn as the rudder bit into the airflow that streamed over it from the propellers, heading away from the shore and the "screaming, frantic men in the boats. Just before one of the crew pulled the hatch shut, Richter saw a boat caught in the BVI38's wash turn over, throwing its struggling occupants into the water.

Its engines roaring, the flying-boat emerged from the shelter of the promontory. Richter, who had followed Kleber on to the flight deck, slipped into the vacant co-pilot's seat and at once felt a wave of relaxation sweep through him. It was as though he was once more now master of his own destiny, seated behind the controls of an aircraft.

The Russian gunners were wide awake and fire crackled round the aircraft as it began its take-off run. Richter, anxious to help, held the throttles fully open, leaving Kleber with both hands free to hold the control column. Kleber nodded his thanks and the flying-boat surged forward, gathering speed slowly, with streams of multi-coloured tracer hosing all around it.

A series of wicked thuds told Richter that the machine was taking hits. He held his breath as the endless seconds went by. The dark water of the lake streamed towards the aircraft's nose, blurring under the hull.

The BV138 bounced once, twice, and then the buffeting stopped as the machine lifted into the air, water cascading from its underside. Fountains of water erupted around it as the Russian tank gunners blazed away, but the shots were wide of the mark. Kleber held the aircraft low down until they were clear of the lake and then climbed out over Spandau, turning gradually north-north-east. Behind him, the gunfire died away.

He flinched as something cold and hard pressed into the back of his neck. It was the muzzle of the woman's Schmeisser. She stood behind his seat and shouted to him above the roar of engines:

'You're heading in the wrong direction. Turn due west. Now!'

She pointed to the compass on the instrument panel, indicating silently that she knew how to read it.

'But that will take us over the Allied lines,' Kleber yelled.

'Precisely! Now do as you are told, and turn!'

Helplessly, Kleber glanced at Richter. The latter nodded emphatically. Crazy, thought Kleber, absolutely crazy. To hell with it. And turned west.

The woman beckoned to the youngest of the three scientists, who had been standing in the entrance to the flight deck, and handed him the Schmeisser.

'If either of these two makes a false move,' she ordered, indicating the pilots, 'shoot him. But for God's sake don't shoot both of them, or we're all in trouble.'

The man nodded. In the last few weeks he had come to trust her implicitly. He took her place behind Kleber, the gun at the ready.

Julia Connors made her way back to the radio operator's position. The airman who manned it was nursing a bullet wound in the shoulder and smiled weakly at her, making no objection when she indicated that she wished to take his place.

Much of the equipment on the radio console was unfamiliar to her, but her SOE radio training now stood her in good stead and it took her only seconds to master the controls of the high-frequency set. It was a powerful piece of equipment, designed to communicate at long ranges over the ocean, and it was in full working order.

She turned the knob of the frequency selector dial, tuning in carefully, praying that SOE's twenty-four-hour listening service was still monitoring the same frequency that had been in force several months earlier, and reached for the Morse key, tapping out a series of coded letters. Part of the code was her personal callsign, the other part referred to the mission on which she had been engaged. That, she thought as she tapped out the code over and over again, ought to make somebody sit up.

Long seconds went by. Then, faintly in her headphones, she heard the dots and dashes of a response. It was her callsign repeated, followed by an interrogative.

Three minutes later, Julia Connors removed the headphones and leaned wearily back in the operator's seat. She had done all she could; the distant listener now knew where she was, and where she was heading. She had ended her message with an urgent request for fighter cover. It should, she calculated, take about ten minutes for a priority signal to reach one of the Allied airfields on the other side of the Elbe, and another five or ten minutes for fighters to get airborne.

She stood up and looked astern through a transparent hatch in the cabin roof. Daylight was already spreading over the eastern sky. With it would come the Russian fighters, patrolling watchfully to the west of Berlin.

The Elbe, and Allied territory, was eighty miles away. She had no idea how long it would take the lumbering flying boat to reach it; half an hour, she thought — forty minutes at the outside. She wondered, fearfully, how long it would be before the Russians found them.

Chapter Twelve

IN THE FLYING-BOAT'S COCKPIT, KLEBER WAS HAVING problems. It was only after he had been airborne for some minutes that the damage the aircraft had sustained became apparent. As the BV138 flew on, the oil pressure warning light suddenly began to glow on the instrument panel; Kleber ordered one of the crew to investigate, and the man reported that both the oil and coolant pipes had been shot through by machine-gun fire. Moreover, one of the aircraft's twin tail-booms was riddled like a sieve. The whole aircraft, in fact, was in such a condition that it was doubtful whether it would continue flying for much longer. There was nothing for it but to hang on and hope for the best, keeping as low as possible. Kleber explained to the woman, who had returned to stand behind him, that he was deviating from a westerly course only so that he could fly from lake to lake; if the machine began to break up he would then at least have a chance of setting it down in one piece.

It was an intermittent trail of white smoke, streaming from the flying-boat's port engine, that first drew the fighter pilots' attention to it. The machine was near Genthin, some forty miles from Berlin, and was creeping steadily westwards, following the line of the Elbe-Havel Canal.

The leader of the three Russian Yak-9s, First Lieutenant Ivan Semyenov, was the first to spot the limping German aircraft. At first he was puzzled, for he had never encountered a machine of this type before; his fifteen victories so far comprised a collection of Messerschmitt 110s, Focke-Wulf 190s and Junkers 88s. But he was familiar with all the Allied types, and he had no doubt that this was an enemy aircraft, even though he was not yet close enough to see the black crosses on its wings.

Semyenov was pleased, now, that he had missed his breakfast in order to take off before dawn in the hope of catching the odd fugitive enemy aircraft trying to slip away northwards through the ever-narrowing corridor between east and west. He did not stop to consider why this particular machine was heading in a westerly direction; the only thought in his mind was that the war would soon be over, and that this might be the last opportunity to add to his score and perhaps earn himself another decoration.

Ordering his two wingmen to remain 'upstairs' as top cover, just in case enemy fighters were lurking in the drifting, patchy cloud that was spreading across the sky from the east, Semyenov went slanting down to make his attack. He smiled with satisfaction, noting that the white smoke trail from his target's engine was growing denser. This one, he thought, should be easy meat.

The BVI38's rear gunner, crouching in his draughty position, saw the threat arrowing down out of the reddish-grey eastern sky and screamed a warning over the intercom. Kleber reacted instinctively, putting the aircraft into a steep turn, feeling its damaged structure creaking and groaning under his hands. In the vibrating fuselage, the passengers who were not already seated were thrown off balance by the sudden manoeuvre. Professor Gorbach fell heavily, banging his head painfully against the fuselage wall, and clung grimly to a metal strut, white-faced with fear.

The Russian fighter matched the flying-boat's sudden turn, its pilot intent on getting the BV138 into his sights. Semyenov was a great advocate of closing the range as much as possible before opening fire; that way, one made a speedy 'kill' more certain. Compared to many fighters the Yak-9 was fairly lightly armed, with one 20-mm cannon and a. single machine-gun, so there was no margin for spraying ammunition wastefully around the sky at extreme range.

It was unfortunate, for Semyenov, that he had not made a more thorough study of the Soviet Air Force's recognition manuals of enemy aircraft. Had he done so, he would have known that, in addition to its machine-guns, a Blohm und Voss BV138 flying-boat was equipped with two 20-mm cannon, one mounted in the nose and the other in the rear gun position: and that the cannon had a far longer effective range than the machine-guns of the enemy bombers he had been used to intercepting.

The sudden unexpected twinkling light in the BVI38's rear turret at extreme range came as a complete shock to him. His finger tensed on the trigger of his own guns, but there was no time — no time, even, for more than a moment of fleeting surprise.

Either the young gunner in the flying-boat was an amazingly good shot or else he was very lucky. Either way, it made no difference. The armoured windscreen of Semyonov's Yak was strong enough to withstand the impact of a machine-gun bullet, but not a 20-mm cannon shell. It exploded inwards and the storm of mingled perspex and steel shell splinters turned the upper half of the pilot's body into a bloody pulp. His hand tightened convulsively on the control column, jerking it backwards, and the Yak went into a steep climb, gaining several hundred feet before losing speed, stalling and flicking over on its back. It dived vertically into the ground and exploded in a bubble of flame, scattering Ivan Semyenov and his dreams over two fields.

The other two Yak pilots saw what had happened with horror and disbelief. Semyenov, to be shot down by this lumbering wreck of an aircraft! With vengeance in their hearts, they dived down to even the score.

At 0520 that morning, Wing Commander George Yeoman had taken off from Celle at the head of a section of four Meteors with much the same intentions as the unfortunate Semyenov — to try and locate any German aircraft passing through the corridor west of Berlin, RAF Intelligence now believed that the enemy had abandoned their intentions of setting up a 'national redoubt' in the mountains of Bavaria and were instead ferrying aircraft north in considerable numbers, possibly to make a final stand in Norway. The bays and estuaries along the north German coast were filled with transport seaplanes, which were being attacked at every possible opportunity by the fighter-bombers of the 2nd Tactical Air Force. At all costs, a mass exodus by enemy forces to Norway had to be prevented; a last stand there might prolong the war in Europe only for three months, four at the outside, but it would entail a further enormous cost in human life.

Yeoman led the formation north-eastwards across the Elbe, following the now-familiar route towards Lübeck. Over on the right the sun was rising, casting long shadows across the ground, and to the right of the sun the smoke of Berlin was clearly visible.

Over Hagenow, Yeoman swung his Meteors towards the south-east at fifteen thousand feet, until they were heading directly for the pall of smoke that hung over the enemy capital. He did not wish to get too close to Berlin, because the city was now firmly a Russian preserve and British and American fighter pilots had been warned to keep clear of it except when flying on specially-authorized sorties of not less than three squadrons. The spectre that haunted the Allied Command was that Allied and Russian air formations might mistake each other for the enemy, with catastrophic effects on what was already a tenuous relationship.

Yeoman had been flying on the new heading for no more than a minute when the urgent instruction from Group Central Control came crackling over the radio — an instruction which, at first, he found difficult to comprehend. Only when the controller repeated it did its full significance sink in.

An enemy flying-boat, carrying very important passengers, had taken off from the vicinity of Berlin thirty minutes earlier and was flying due west at low level. Yeoman's orders were to intercept it and escort it safely into Allied territory as far as Steinhuder Lake, north-west of Hannover.

Yeoman's mind raced. 'Very important passengers', the controller had said. What could it mean? Some top-ranking enemy generals, perhaps, flying west to negotiate a surrender? Maybe one of the *very* top Nazis, such as Himmler — or even ... no, that was unthinkable.

Yeoman, who unlike Ivan Semyenov had made it his business for years to study data on every type of German aircraft, did some rapid mental calculations, looking at his map as he did so. He knew that a BV138 flying-boat — assuming that it was, in fact, such a type they were looking for — could do about 170 mph flat out, but a speed of about 150 mph at low altitude would probably be more realistic. If it had been airborne for thirty minutes, that ought to put it ... his finger traced a line on the map, running west from Berlin, and stopped near Gardelegen.

Gardelegen was thirty miles from their present position. Crisply, he ordered his pilots to turn on to a new heading of 190 degrees and increase speed. As one, the four Meteors tilted into a shallow dive and sped towards their rendezvous.

In the BV138, Kleber and Richter were both exerting pressure on the twin control columns, turning this way and that to avoid the savage attacks of the two Russian fighters. The recipe for survival was to stay as low as possible, to keep the big machine turning just above the treetops, so that the attackers could not come up from underneath. Nevertheless, the two pilots knew that they could not hope to keep this up for much longer; the flying-boat had already taken more hits in the wings and every fresh tight manoeuvre threatened to shake it to pieces. Moreover, the gallant rear gunner had been wounded in the shoulder, and although he was still firing back he was almost in a state of collapse through loss of blood.

Every new turning manoeuvre, too, meant that time was being lost. The Allied lines were still twenty miles way. Both Kleber and Richter knew that they might just as well have been on the moon.

The Russian fighters were coming in again, this time from different directions. The German pilots turned hard to face one of them, which fired wide of the mark and hurtled overhead with only feet to spare.

The other fighter was jockeying for position several hundred metres astern. In the rear turret, the 20-mm cannon thudded briefly, then fell silent. Weakly, the wounded rear gunner called over the intercom:

'I'm out of ammunition! The enemy fighter is at four hundred metres and closing. Break starboard on my signal — my God!'

'What is it? Kleber almost screamed. 'What's happening?' Without waiting for the gunner to reply, he hauled the flying-boat round to the right, narrowly avoiding a line of high-tension cables that flashed under its wingtip. He was in time to catch a fleeting glimpse of a silvery shape streaking across the sky at phenomenal speed.

'He went straight across the Russian's bows,' the gunner shouted. 'Threw the Ivan right off his aim! There are three — no, four of them. They look a bit like Me 262s, but they aren't. I've never seen anything like them before!'

Out of the side cockpit window Richter saw two more of the strange aircraft harassing the second Russian fighter, diving past it at high speed. The Yak-9, flimsy by comparison, was buffeted like a leaf in their slipstream.

'Meteors!' Richter yelled. 'They're British Meteor jets, and they're keeping the Ivans off our tail! Kleber, tell your gunners not to fire on them!'

The Yaks were considerably more manoeuvrable than the British jets, but the Russian pilots were given no opportunity to use this advantage. The Meteors split up into pairs and continued to make high-speed passes at the Russians, who — after one of them had almost stalled into the ground — eventually gave up and sped away eastwards at top speed.

The flying-boat resumed its course and the four Meteors slotted into tight formation on either side, the pilots throttling back to safe low cruising speed and lowering their flaps to keep pace with the German aircraft. Out of his window, Richter could clearly see the helmeted head of the nearest British pilot, the man's face turned towards him. A moment later the Englishman raised a hand and made a series of jabbing motions with his finger, pointing straight ahead. Richter acknowledged with a wave.

A few minutes later the formation crossed the front line without incident. South of Celle, the Meteors broke away with a waggle of their wings and their place was taken immediately by a flight of Spitfires. As the shark-like shapes tucked themselves in alongside the flying boat, Richter felt an involuntary surge of panic, but it quickly passed. Never again, he thought, would a Spitfire confront him in combat.

Von Gleiwitz came forward on to the flight deck and Kleber asked him how the passengers were.

'Sick,' von Gleiwitz replied. 'The old chap isn't looking very well at all, but I expect he's all right.'

'Any more casualties among the crew?'

'No, just the gunner, and he'll pull through all right. The woman is patching him up. She's a bloody marvel — stayed as cool as ice all the time you were throwing the aircraft around.'

He looked anxiously out of the cockpit, at the gaping holes in the wing and the smoking engine.

'Are we going to make it?'

Kleber glanced at him and smiled reassuringly. 'Two of the engines are overheating, one of them is in danger of bursting into flames at any moment, we're all shot to hell — but yes, we'll make it.'

He pointed ahead through the windscreen. A few miles away, past the sprawling grey patch that was Hannover, the glistening expanse of Steinhuder Lake rose through the morning mist.

Epilogue

JOACHIM RICHTER SAT DESPONDENTLY IN A SMALL, CELL-LIKE room in the British military headquarters in the shattered city of Hannover. Beyond the barred window, military vehicles rolled along the street in a never-ending throb of sound. The door of the room was open and an armed sentry stood there, in such a position that he could see the Luftwaffe officer at all times. Von Gleiwitz and Kleber, Richter had no doubt, were confined in similar rooms elsewhere, awaiting interrogation.

At least the British had treated him with scrupulous fairness, if not friendliness. They had removed none of his personal belongings, not even his two remaining cheroots and his lighter. He lit one of the precious cheroots now and idly watched the smoke as it curled up towards the chipped ceiling, lapsing into a reverie. He deliberately avoided thinking about what the future might have in store for him.

The sound of the sentry coming noisily to attention made him look up. A man in the uniform of a Royal Air Force officer stood framed in the doorway.

Richter stood up as the man stepped into the room. The stranger snapped up a brief salute and Richter replied with a click of his heels and a fractional bow.

The stranger — a Wing Commander and a much-decorated pilot, as Richter could see — came forward and stood face to face with him, surveying him intently. After a few moments of silence, he spoke in a very quiet voice, as though talking to himself.

'So, you are Colonel Richter.'

'Yes, Wing Commander. You seem to be well informed.'

The other looked faintly surprised at the German's command of the English language, then smiled disarmingly and reached into a pocket of his tunic. He pulled out a much-creased photograph, and held it out so that Richter could see it. Astonished, Richter recognized his own features.

The RAF officer took out a pipe, inspected the tobacco and applied a match to it. Through the smoke, he gazed at the German.

'I've been following your fortunes', he said, 'with considerable interest. I understand you've flown Messerschmitt 262s. I'd like to know all about that.'

Richter immediately became evasive. 'I cannot answer any of your questions, Wing Commander. The war is not yet over.'

The other smiled. 'It is for you.'

'For me, yes. But not for many others. Not yet.'

The Wing Commander opened his mouth to speak, but was interrupted by a polite cough from the doorway. He turned and saw a British Army major, wearing the green flashes of the Intelligence Corps.

'There you are, sir,' the major said. 'I've been looking for you. I wonder if you'd mind coming with me? It is important.'

The RAF officer nodded and moved towards the door. Just before he left the room, he turned and faced Richter again, removing his pipe from his mouth, and smiled.

'We shall talk again, Colonel,' he said. 'Another time, and in another place. I have a feeling we have a great deal in common.'

'Wing Commander!'

'Yes. What is it?'

'You appear to know my name. May I know yours?'

'Yeoman.' And then the wing commander was gone, leaving Richter staring at the open doorway, and the sentry just beyond it.

Yeoman accompanied the Intelligence Corps major down a long corridor, to another part of the building. The major made a sudden remark that puzzled his companion.

'I thought for a minute that you'd forgotten the reason you were asked to come here, sir.'

Yeoman looked at him. 'What are you talking about? I came to talk to Colonel Richter, to help interrogate him, if you like. And you've just dragged me away.'

The major stopped dead in his tracks. 'Good God! You mean no one has told you?'

The man looked fearfully embarrassed. 'Look,' he said, fighting hard to curb his impatience, 'I haven't the faintest notion what you're talking about. Told me what?'

'Well, sir, it's the lady — the one in Room 29. She came out of Berlin with the Germans, sir. You were to be taken straight to see her on the orders of an Air Commodore Sampson.'

The name struck a strident chord in Yeoman's memory. An iciness crept over him as unwanted memories crowded into his mind.

The major hesitated, then said: 'She's been through a lot, sir, and should be resting. As soon as she arrived here, she asked us about you, and when she learned that you were here in Germany she lost control completely — broke down and became practically hysterical. She wouldn't let anyone give her a sedative, though. Just kept insisting on seeing you.'

Yeoman's mind was in a turmoil. Harshly, he ordered the major to take him to Room 29. It was in a wing of the building that had been turned into an improvized hospital, and there were two people outside the door. One was an army nurse, the other an armed guard who, like the major, wore Intelligence Corps flashes.

Yeoman identified himself and the nurse smiled at him, reaching for the door handle.

'Don't stay too long, sir. She ought really to be asleep.'

Still uncomprehending, Yeoman pushed the door fully open and stood on the threshold, emotions chasing one another across his face as he stared for long moments at the room's sole occupant.

Her face was drawn and lined, but it was still hers. Wordlessly, Julia reached out to him. Yeoman stepped into the room, quietly closing the door behind him.

Printed in Great Britain
by Amazon